THE C

Ravi Mangla

Spuyten Duyvil
New York City

Library of Congress Cataloging-in-Publication Data

Names: Mangla, Ravi, 1988-, author.
Title: The observant / Ravi Mangla.
Description: New York City : Spuyten Duyvil, [2022]
Identifiers: LCCN 2022003610 | ISBN 9781956005585 (paperback)
Subjects: LCGFT: Novels. | Political fiction.
Classification: LCC PS3613.A53696 O27 2022 | DDC 813/.6--dc23/eng/20220321
LC record available at https://lccn.loc.gov/2022003610

"I've often noticed that we are not able to look at what we have in front of us, unless it's inside a frame."

Abbas Kiarostami

It took less than an hour for the city noise to be displaced by silence. There was something perverse about how abruptly the city ended, its industry and development brought to a heel. I listened for familiar sounds—sounds that I knew as part of a larger sonic architecture—but nothing registered. The two men on either side of me spoke in hushed tones. I caught the odd whiff of English that filtered into their conversation (references to nineties hip-hop artists, European soccer clubs, Hollywood blockbusters). Dried perspiration from the hood anointed each breath, and I tried consciously to slow my breathing, subsist on as little oxygen as possible. I thought of the Taoist monks that took fewer than a single breath each minute, the product of years of austere practice. (Paced breaths may be the ultimate form of self-denial.) The car veered onto unpaved road. Loose gravel crunched underneath the tires. I started to reach into my pocket, a stress reflex, but thought better of it. Without explanation or forewarning the men placed their hands on my shoulders and forced me onto the floor. One of them plunged a knee into my lower back, pinning me in a facedown position. I refrained from protesting or resisting his physical weight. The car slowed and a hand tapped at the window. The glass was

7

lowered and *salaams* were exchanged. I tried to follow the arc of their conversation. The driver spoke in abbreviated sentences, pruning his answers, as though the same questions had been asked at the checkpoint previous. His inquisitor sounded young, pliant; he hadn't yet assumed that cold, unassailable authority that passed like a toxin through contact with the uniform. After no more than a minute, the window was sealed and the car continued toward its destination. I waited to be returned to my seat, for the knee to release me from the carpet, but the pressure only increased.

~

Ali poured half the dispenser of maple syrup on his pancakes, until his plate was a pool of slow-moving amber. Once he had finished pouring he slipped his finger across the nose of the dispenser and deposited it in his mouth with a soft moan of gratification.

I wondered how hygienic the gesture was, but I wasn't about to question his etiquette, especially when he was here at my behest.

"So I imagine you've heard the news," he said. "Mohadessi is calling for the seizure of all media he deems a danger to the state."

"I'm not overly bothered."

"Aren't you?" he said, staring pensively in the polished reflecting pool. "Perhaps you should be."

Ali was a former mid-level official in the Ministry of Culture who was dismissed when his reformist views no longer hewed to the hardline base. Now he owned a second-hand bookstore in the city. We met through a mutual friend, a producer of one of my early projects. It was clear his revolutionary leanings ran deeper than paternal sympathies. But I didn't ask how he occupied his free time and he didn't offer suggestions.

"What brings you to our little authoritarian oasis at this time of year?"

"Background for a new project."

"A riveting summary."

I elaborated: "I'm interviewing the activists behind SILO."

"How may I ask do you plan to manage that sleight of hand?"

"I hoped that you might be able to make an introduction," I said, pausing to provide the request with the proper weight.

He made a tisking sound. The waiter came around and refilled our coffee cups.

"And here I was thinking this was a social call."

"What are my chances of getting an audience?"

Ali looked at the table beside us, a young couple meticulously subdividing an oversized waffle for their infant child.

"Not impossible." he paused. "But not particularly likely either. They don't covet the attention."

He removed from his jacket pocket a paperback novel and marked down in the margins a short note. The illustrations on the front cover suggested science fiction of an interplanetary variety.

"And if they agree to meet?"

"And in the unlikely event that they agree to meet with you, the rest will be taken care of."

He scooped a forkful of pancake and marshaled it into his mouth, and then looked down at the untouched breakfast in front of me.

"Don't order oatmeal next time. It depresses me."

~

They placed me on a threadbare couch and removed the hood. The room was not the spartan undercroft I was anticipating. Instead, they had delivered me to a sunlit country house with checkered curtains, handwoven blankets, and other homespun furnishings. A slight man, short of forty, sat across from me in a wooden rocking chair. His head was barren and beard sheared to shadow. Rounded glasses were pinned to the pocket of his white linen shirt. A fleet of naval vessels, preserved in glass bottles, were arranged above his head (a curious collection in a landlocked country). He issued a directive in Arabic. The other men rose and retired to the adjoining room.

"I hope you can forgive us for taking your phone." He handed it back to me, undamaged at first glance. "We must take the necessary precautions."

I waited for him to continue, but he seemed content to idle in the mutual silence, his chair rocking softly on the sheepskin rug.

"Would you like a cup of tea?"

Before I had provided my answer, he proceeded to pour two cups from the earthenware pot on the table. The scent of peppermint perfumed the room.

"Mr. Rai, I must profess, I'm an admirer of your work. Especially your film on the Philadelphia bombing. This is one of the reasons we agreed to meet with you," he said. "While some of my colleagues have apprehensions, I believe there is value in speaking with creators such as yourself. Our aims are not so different after all. Both are rooted in a desire to bring the cruelties of the past to light."

"I suppose that's true."

"But your audience is diffuse. They're not governed by the same borders as ours, the same painful legacy. While we may be the cradle of life, it feels as though we're forever in our infancy."

I took a sip of tea, which seemed to steady my nerves after the lengthy car ride. My neck and shoulders eased.

"Do you know anything about epigenetics?" he asked.

"Very little," I said, truthfully.

"Trauma is a birthmark that can be passed from one generation to the next. It proves that our history is part of us," he said. "You see, before I became politically disposed, it was decided I would become a doctor—as my father was, and his father before him. My first medical posting was in a refugee camp along the southern border. I imagined myself as a savior of a kind. But when I stopped telling people what I thought they needed and started listening, it became clear that what ailed them was not illness born of the body, but a crisis of spirit. I remember an old woman with arthritic symptoms. We conducted test after test, but each one showed her to be in optimal health. Later, I learned more about her: she wasn't able to read or write but had, within her small town, become an expert at identifying bone fragments."

"An anthropologist by necessity."

"Indeed."

"May I ask why you chose not to protect your identity?" I asked.

"How can we incite others to act without fear if we ourselves are servants to it? Fear is ultimately what we are fighting—fear wielded as an instrument of control. It's the one quality that weds the poor and the corrupt," he said. "For many Mohadessi is the benevolent father who delivers his lessons with the back of his hand. But if they could only see the profiteering that happens at their expense. The deals with petroleum companies and land developers. Funds diverted from public services that are never recovered."

"Do you have records of this?"

"We have records of all of it. The sums spent on private planes and luxury hotels. Tailored suits flown in from Europe. The mistresses secreted away in penthouse suites. Male masseurs summoned at four in the morning. Our politicians, for all their financial guile, are dreadfully poor at securing their accounts."

"If that's the case, why not leak the documents?"

He lifted a finger up to his lips.

"We must begin in silence. Imagine how easy would it be for Mohadessi to hold your people responsible for falsifying the documents. It wouldn't be such an implausible claim, after all. Information is a source of considerable power and we cannot be too quick to surrender it."

He leaned forward in his seat and decanted into my cup the remaining tea, now cool to the touch.

"Revolutions are vulnerable to the same sort of exceptionalism as the autocrats they seek to depose," he continued. "This is a struggle that has been waged thousands of times before, and we won't be the last ones. We cannot assume that just because a person grew up under the thumb of this regime they will be standing beside us. Belief has to be kindled among those whose faith has faltered."

"That was the reasoning behind the midnight rice deliveries."

"What better way to deliver literature than inside bags of rice. We were inspired by the breakfasts of your Black Panthers," he said. "The media will portray us as heathens, occasioning mayhem for no reason. We are not blind to this fact. Our largest media company is owned by Mohadessi's cousin. New channels of communication must be carved out to deliver information to the people. This requires time."

"And shovels."

He nodded his head.

"When would you like to begin filming?"

I angled my phone against the ceramic teapot: a makeshift camera stand.

"Right now."

They dropped me in the heart of the city, some blocks from the hotel. The sun bore down, its heat clinging to weary pedestrians like a lead vest. Vendors closed up their sidewalk kiosks and cars struggled for purchase in the overburdened traffic. The scent of diesel permeated, its industrial cologne both intoxicating and oppressive. I waited for the light to change and when it didn't I crossed anyway. At the street corner two children, returning from school, taunted a stray dog with fried treats. Headless mannequins postured in storefront windows, dressed in fashions that one might describe as puritanical chic. I passed underneath a stretch of scaffolding, which brought a welcome respite from the searing heat. Splinters of glass perked up in the sunlight. Motorbikes weaved expertly through the cramped traffic, immune to the constraints of size. I considered how long it would take to achieve some measure of assurance in this setting, the grim illusion of personal safety. Bodies filed past me, mindful to avoid even the suggestion of physical contact. Posters for a large fireworks celebration were wheat-pasted to the sides of buildings: a convenient cover for the flaking paint and battered concrete. A woman lost her footing stepping off the bus. Several oranges tumbled from her shopping bag, alighting on the narrow cracks in the sidewalk.

~

In the refuge of the hotel room I reviewed the footage from the morning. The lighting was less than exemplary, but I wasn't about to agonize over technical shortcomings. The improvised quality, I imagined, would be part of the charm. (Plus, the worst of it could be remedied in the editing room.)

I made a handshake agreement with the SILO activists not to share the footage—neither with my story editor nor producer—until after the upcoming religious holiday. Once the video was uploaded onto an outside storage account, saved under a code name (the title of my favorite Tarkovsky film), I cleared the file from my phone's memory. In the background a news program cycled on the state-run network, lavishing praise on Mohadessi's plan to provide dental checkups for every child in the country, painting him as a protector of the public welfare.

I took a break from parsing the footage to order dinner from the hotel restaurant. I requested a tomato and basil omelette from off the menu. Moments after the order was placed the phone sounded. I suspected the restaurant was calling back to amend the order (out of fresh basil, if I had to guess), but the caller on the end of the line remained quiet. There was no static signal or menacing breath. Only silence. I set the phone down in its cradle and went to take a shower.

The water was restoring, and I lingered in its warmth for longer than I would normally feel entitled in my own apartment. I toweled off and changed into clothes for sleep. A table tennis match was on the television. Two men in condensed shorts and crew socks whipped an orange ball across a small table. The scene lent itself to comedy, but their expressions conveyed a fierce zealotry, as though the lives of their children were hanging in the balance. There was a sound of rolling wheels followed by a timid knock, barely audible over the television. I unchained the door and the server backed the dining cart into the room. He shunned eye contact upon entering. With silverware nested inside the folded napkin, he set down the tray on a side table. I handed him a modest tip, noticing for the first time that his hand was wrapped in a loose cotton bandage. He slid the gratuity into his pocket.

"Is there anything else?" I asked.

He hesitated for several seconds, his eyes welded to the floor. Perspiration jeweled above his brow. He wheeled the cart out of the room and closed the door behind him. I lifted the silver cloche concealing the platter. The omelette was cold and absent—as far as I could tell—of both the tomato and the basil. I removed with my fork a slice of omelette, rotated it as if on a rotisserie spit, and then set down the utensil. Without taking a bite, I deposited the silver tray in the hallway: a midnight snack for a famished sleepwalker.

~

Once the city was a vision, birthed where the river split into two. All wildflower and thistle. A Hellenistic settlement that fell to the Parthians, who banished their political adversaries to its provinces. The exiles, in turn, erected granite monuments and white marble archways, corbelled bridges and manicured gardens. A rigorous process of jurisprudence was adopted in which citizens of all standing were given equal weight under the law. Public forums afforded a voice to the lowliest of denizen. When bordering states, ravaged by disease and political discord, received word of its splendor, they conspired to oust its populace and occupy the city in their stead—an undertaking they accomplished with marvelous ease.

The city, by virtue of its location, emerged as a principal trading post on the Silk Road, renowned for its muskmelon, dyes, and the most fragrant of resins. In less than half a century, the population doubled. Sailors and merchants traveled from near and far to market their wares. Genghis Khan was rumored to have witnessed a meteor shower above the city, considered this an omen, and resolved instead to plunder the next town over.

A series of earthquakes in the twelfth and thirteenth centuries leveled much of its former opulence. Famine and plague under the Ilkhans led to mass displacement and a steep decline in population. Marco Polo, as the legend goes, on his return to Venice, buried his most beloved horse at its borders.

It wasn't until the Safavids staked their claim to the city that it entered a period of convalescence. Universities and cultural institutions cropped up around the region and many of its former monuments were restored. The city was renamed by the presiding caliph, christened after the mountains that crowned its borders. British troops occupied the city during the First World War, many of whom remained to dowse for minerals and metals. The discovery of vast reserves of oil in the first half of the twentieth century resulted in a power tussle between British and Russian forces for command of the region.

In succeeding decades a mass movement to expel foreign influences and nationalize the country's resources reached critical mass. During this period the capital was resettled in the city and a provisional constitution was enshrined: the first of its kind.

The United States, under the pretense of deepening Communist sympathies, used their authority in the region to mount a counter revolution. The puppet government foisted the English language upon school age children and signed contracts with American corporations to siphon oil from untapped lands. The confidence game was short-lived and soon, following a successful military coup, the country entered a state of martial law. It remained under the charge of its military head until his death seven years later, at which point the charismatic young politician Mohammad Mohadessi rose to power, vowing to restore the national identity. By the time the next elections arrived, he had declared himself president for life.

~

After a breakfast of coffee and toast, I stopped at the barbershop for a hot shave, an extravagance I indulged in once or twice a month. No other customers were in the queue. The barber—a short man with gray curls like coiled springs—seemed almost startled by my presence. I gestured to the stubble around my jaw line, an easy game of charades. He placed me in the chair, adjusted the seat height, and whisked a silken apron around my shoulders. I noticed a soapstone resting on a neatly folded prayer rug, and I tried to imagine this man worshipping here, prone on the checkered floor, surrounded by sacrificial locks of hair.

His right hand tremored as he dispensed the lather. The foam was applied to my face with a stiff-bristled brush. The previous summer several hairdressers were raided, their owners fined or imprisoned, for molding hair in the style of a certain androgynous pop singer. This was undoubtedly not one of those groomers.

He unfurled the straight razor and held it eye level, making some inscrutable measurement. I stared at the water damage above me, the rust-colored stains in baroque patterns, spanning the length of the ceiling. He made his maiden stroke, the sound like sandpaper, and then bathed the knife in a bowl of cool water.

He took an uncommonly long time to make the second stroke. The radio on the table was tuned to white noise. The blade followed the curve of my neck, moving against the grain, before nicking the skin. I felt the blood forming beneath my chin. He dipped the razor into the basin. We watched the water turn deep red.

Sunni peered through the parted door before letting me in. (I half-expected to be asked for a password.) Mind you, I didn't blame him. Three years of house arrest would wear away at anyone's nerves. It was a wonder he didn't speak in tongues, collect nail clippings in a jar.

Naya, his wife, greeted me briefly, distantly, and then disappeared into her studio. She was a sculptor that worked with sheet metal and vacuum-formed plastics. Her work was sought after by foreign collectors. Part of me envied their arrangement. Two people living in shared solitude, taking meals in their studios, communing for sleep and the occasional cup of tea. I imagined, under those circumstances, my own marriage might have found its footing.

Sunni wrote a book about an affair between a college professor and his student, which amassed quite a bit of acclaim in Europe. The Cultural Minister branded it as lecherous, debauched art, and sentenced him to five years of house arrest, along with a twelve year ban on publishing his writing. The international arts community decried the ruling. Petitions were circulated (as petitions are wont to do), but here the author remained, a plastic monitor clamped around his ankle, the shackle pulsing with green light.

We sat in his office, a small cubiform room overlooking a tree-lined street. His desk faced the open window. He looked older, tired, in his unironed shirt.

I asked him if he was getting any work done.

"Work," he repeated, rolling the word around in his head. "You would think the terms of the punishment would yield creative fruits, but mostly I find the time paralyzing. Each morning I memorize a new type of bird—its Latin name, habitat, physical characteristics. Then I translate these attributes into Farsi, and then into French, and finally into Urdu. There is no purpose to the undertaking, no end game. It's an exercise in presence, a way to move along the hours. The routine anchors me. It gives shape to the day."

"Does Naya know about this?"

"I don't wish to burden Naya with my debilities. She has had to deal with enough. It was my writing that put her own career at risk. Some galleries won't touch her work. I'm still unable to forgive myself for that."

A bird lands on the sill of the window: white-breasted with dark blue feathers.

"*Delichon urbicum*"

"What does that translate to?"

"I'm not an ornithologist."

"Will you leave the country at the end of the sentence?"

He seemed confused by the question, turned back from the window.

"No."

"Why not?"

"Because it's home."

~

The national fireworks celebration happened to fall on Mohadessi's birthday. Perhaps it was a matter of chance. I walked uptown, toward the residential corridors of the city. The government broadcast American cartoons on its network (copiously edited) to keep children indoors after dark. Still, I saw many kids holding sparklers out the windows of cramped high-rise tenements, almost as a show of solidarity. The festivities were less mediated than the celebrations of my youth. Loud bursts and whistles sounded from distant quarters. I rounded a corner where several teenagers were tossing firecrackers into a blazing trash can. Phosphorescent clouds fanned through the air, dense with sulfurous fumes. I approached a park in which dozens of locals had gathered. I forded through the enraptured crowd, knocking between bodies. At the center of the pack, two men in hooded sweatshirts were preparing to launch a barrel-shaped incendiary. An older man at my side offered me a rolled slip of paper, which I had naively assumed was a joint, before recognizing it rightly as a hand-rolled cigarette. I declined the offering. The fuse was lit and the two men moved backwards with reluctant steps. The projectile seared skyward and ruptured into fractals of sapphire light. The explosion was followed by a scattering of applause. I withdrew from the crowd and drifted to the periphery of the park. On a nearby bench, a young woman sobbed, encircled by a consoling cabinet of friends. The flag on her right cheek, drawn with grease paint, was smeared. I turned down a tapered side street. Teenagers shuffled into darkened buildings, retiring for the night. The sound of fireworks became less pronounced, and the intervals between bursts grew longer. I heard dogs barking in the distance. A delivery van passed, its headlights illuminating the full width of the street. Several yards ahead of me was a man in a starched white shirt and windbreaker. He was leaning against the hood of a parked car, maintaining eye contact with me. His hands were in his pockets and there was something about his posture that unnerved me. I turned back toward the hotel. The steady rhythm of footsteps followed, filling the silence. I walked at a quicker clip, only to hear the shadow behind me match my pace. (Was I falling prey to an unfounded paranoia? Once in Southeast Asia, I had been threatened, held at knifepoint, by an interview subject who felt they had been deceived by my questions, but never had I been tracked or followed.) I hoped to pass an open storefront or public park, to disappear into the anonymity of gathered bodies, but the celebrations were petering and many of the lights in the apartment windows had been extinguished. I merged onto an arterial road. I could still sense him at my heels, his accelerating gait. Revelers passed in the opposite direction. I flinched as a firecracker was tossed from the upper stories. The agitators laughed and hollered down at us. A bus stopped at the corner and I promptly boarded. The bus unfolded its passenger door and continued onward. The profile of the man flickered past the bus. He didn't wave down the vehicle or raise his fist in anger. This left me to doubt my state of alarm. I took a seat beside an elderly man in a mint green shower cap. He held a silver tuning fork in his wizened hand. With each exhalation of the bus, he thrummed the instrument against his knee, the sound sending tremors up the back of my seat.

~

Once back in the hotel room, I unscrewed the underside of my laptop, removed the battery in my phone. I checked that nothing has been tampered with or tacked to the hardware. I glanced inside drawers, closets, underneath the lamp shade, not entirely clear on what I was looking for. I poured the contents of my backpack onto the bed. None of my possessions—as far as I could tell—had been altered or stolen. I called the front desk and requested a car be ready in ten minutes. Then I dialed the airline and booked the next flight out, an hour from now, to the city of Hamburg. (I knew no one in Hamburg, had only been there once before, but it seemed like a sensible location to plot my next move.) This left me only a few minutes to pack my belongings. I started balling clothes and tossing them into the bottom of the suitcase, as though crushed paper into a waste bin. In the bathroom I zippered my shaving kit and toothbrush, rinsed my face with cool water. I gathered my bags and left the room, drops of water still collecting at my chin.

A yellow van waited at the curb, headlights aglow. I loaded two bags into the trunk and settled into the back seat.

"Airport," I said, gesturing with my flattened hand as if it were a plane at take-off.

He nodded and untangled us from the hotel roundabout.

A brief search for the seat belt was abandoned. It was nearing eleven o'clock. Some street lamps remained illuminated, but otherwise it was utterly dark. The driver turned on the radio: traditional music, played in a key that was grating to my uncalibrated ears. He hummed along, his hand gliding lightly over the steering wheel. An image of his children—or who I assumed to be his children—was tacked on the dashboard. A beaded necklace, similar to a rosary, hung from the rearview mirror.

I closed my eyes and imagined lying with my wife Sanne, in a hotel room in Germany, her hand resting on my chest, rising and falling with my breath. I missed the way our bodies intersected, attuned to one another, during hours of sleep. It had been months since I last saw her, and longer since we slept beside each other. In any bed, I felt like half of something that was once whole.

At a stilled intersection the cab slowed. The driver turned to me, a beseeching look on his face. What did he want me to say? Behind us, a car door slammed. I turned around. Two men walked toward the cab, their black car stalled in the middle of the street. They opened both rear doors. My body was rendered immobile with terror. The man on the passenger's side wrested me from the car and secured my wrists with zip ties. His partner slipped over my head a black cover, and together they coerced me into the trunk of their vehicle. I thought suddenly of my luggage, my laptop and phone. (Petty concerns, surely, but objects stocked with personal information.) The trunk door was closed. I kicked at the trunk and yelled for help. Without so much as a word, the recitation of rights, the engine started.

~

Sanne and I attended the opening of a friend's solo exhibition at a Chelsea gallery. The centerpiece of the exhibition, which was situated in the heart of the gallery space, was a white cargo van. The interior of the van was dressed from floor to ceiling in decorative textiles. Concealed speakers relayed stories and folklore from the homes and villages of migratory workers who had died in transport across the border, deprived of food or water. Participants climbed into the back of the van and the doors were shut behind them. When it was our turn to experience it, I felt a panic sweep over me and hammered on the doors until I was let out. The gallery owner plied us with water and snacks in his back office. Sanne pressed her hand to the back of my neck, my body still trembling.

"I don't know what happened," I said to her.

Once I had regained my composure, the gallerist asked if we would be interested in purchasing a piece from the show.

~

The guard watched intently as I stripped down and changed into a navy blue jumpsuit. The color seemed counterintuitive, too ordinary for the context. Prisoners back home were outfitted in orange so they could be identified at a distance, shelled by snipers if the carnage could be justified (which it seemed it always could be).

I was led silently to my cell down a narrow corridor. The guard's boots whined against the floor, which were slick with mop water. We passed leaden doors, one row after another. None of the doors had windows or numbers. The guard led me up a metal staircase, prodded me with the butt of his wooden baton when my pace slowed. They had taken away my *kara*, the silver bracelet native to Sikhs that had been given to me by my late father.

We paused in front of a gray door, unmarked, identical to the others. He urged me inside and then closed the door. I began to yell: yelled until my body had been hollowed and temples throbbed—an intensity of expression untapped since childhood. Weakened, I sat down on the mattress, thin and abraded, and surveyed my accommodations, which were no larger than a walk-in closet. The toilet was deprived of both a seat and cover; the sink basin was rusted. There was no desk or writing surface of any kind. The corner window, covered with iron slats, projected a barcode of light. The room had a souring smell, like that of milk left out overnight. A wiry spider, for whom the cell might be considered spacious, skittered across the concrete floor before holing up inside the toe of my slipper.

Physical isolation proved less of a menace than the utter absence of sound. To be separated from the rest of civilization, without the instruments of communication we took for granted, seemed an insufferable punishment. Sometimes I coughed just to hear the sound reverberate, die away. I had, in the months prior grown accustomed to falling asleep to mundane sounds playing on my phone: rain patter, distant thunder, crackling fires, and the like. The sounds seemed to settle me after long and confounding days cadging money from mercurial investors. As I fell asleep, I tried to remember popular songs from my youth, but either I couldn't remember the lyrics or they played out of key. Meals in the prison were not designed to resolve the hunger. Thin stews, vegetable purees, stale breads. They were served through a mail-sized slot in the door, three times per day. The sound of the metal door sliding open was similar to that of a knife being sharpened, and yet I waited eagerly for this threatening sound, for the grate to open and the outside world to make its meager offering.

~

A pair of studio lights directed their twin ire at my sedentary form. Each light was canted at a forty-five degree angle and both seemed vulnerable to topple at any moment. My inquisitor was seated between the lights, against the far wall. The tableau reminded me of school photos, only without the discharge of a flash or the companionable appeal for a half smile.

I could make out only the broad strokes of his appearance: close cropped hair and the hint of a mustache. A manila folder was opened in his lap.

"Dear Mr. Rai, it gives me no pleasure to have to interview you today," he started, as if delegating a letter to an assistant. "I hope we can sort out this misunderstanding and send you on your way home."

He turned over a page, browsed its backside, and then restored it to its original order.

"We only wish to know where you were between 10 A.M. and 5 P.M. on Wednesday the fifth."

I blinked at the ceiling. The lights left blood orange impressions on the underside of my eyelids.

"By all means take your time."

His blind stabs at empathy felt like an affront to my faculties. A tactic designed for a less perceptive person. He clicked and unclicked his pen against his left knee. The lights persuaded several beads of sweat to form along my upper lip. They made a droning noise I hadn't noticed at first: an insect-like buzzing that scuttled its way into my ear canal and settled there. After an extended silence, the inquisitor spoke up.

"Perhaps you are still exhausted from the ordeal. This is understandable. Let us plan to speak again soon."

He closed the folder in his lap without ceremony.

"How are your accommodations?" he added.

"The nights get very cold."

He stood. Initially I thought he would stalk toward me, but he unlocked the latch above the door handle and whispered to the guard outside. The guard nodded and withdrew himself. A moment later he returned with a folded stack of blankets.

The thin mattress doubled over readily, without resistance. I climbed onto the cushion and drew myself eye level with the window. The pinstriped opening afforded a compromised view of the prison's boundaries: the tall limestone wall crowned with loose coils of wire. Low hills of parched grass peered out over the barricades, beyond which stood a city I couldn't see, and farther still a home I couldn't reach.

A white lookout tower, no larger than my cell, pinnacled the high wall. Through the window, I could see a guard, rifle in hand, staring languidly over the grounds. Were he to look toward the prison quarters, could he distinguish me through the small window? Would he raise his radio to his mouth and signal the guards to storm in and restrain me? Lock me in an even smaller room bereft of light? I mourned the authority exerted by my camera. It was a power I sensed the first time I stepped into a college film class. For a shy child raised by bitterly disappointed people, the camera offered a way to mediate the world. It gave me purpose when I had none. The camera was my armor. Behind the lens I was immune to the ritual indignities of daily life. Now the dynamic had shifted: I was the subject, surveilled by a revolving door of expressionless men in military costumes. My narrative was no longer my own. Whatever was to happen to me was out of my control. I was a goldfish in a glass bowl, looking out on an indifferent world.

~

Sometime at night I was woken by a knock. The guard unlocked the door, waited for me to take the cue to join him outside the cell. He secured the heavy door and led us down the unlit corridor. Down a series of stairs and into an unadorned room, windowless, throbbing with fluorescent lights. A tall man in a double-breasted suit stood before a solitary table and chair, his hands interlaced in front of his waist. On the table was a telephone (beige, plastic shell, from the age of orange shag carpets and wood paneling) and two typed sheets of paper, one next to the other. I sat down in the chair. The first sheet listed two phone numbers, both of which I recognized instantaneously: one was the number for my mother's home in Upstate New York; the other was my wife's cell phone. (They didn't know that we were separated, but then again how would they know such information?) The next sheet was a clumsily written phone script, rife with ungainly phrases and missing articles, which seemed—in its peculiar syntax—more

35

likely to arouse suspicion than assuage it. The script, which placed me in a remote village with limited access to phone and internet, was recited verbatim. To my immeasurable relief, both Sanne and my mother's phones shunted me to voicemail. After recording the same counterfeit message, I was guided back through the dark into the waiting arms of my cell.

~

The only other time I was arrested, sequestered in a jail cell, was at a film festival in the Upper Midwest. An older Black filmmaker known for his independent streak was being hassled by a police officer for smoking within ten feet of the hotel entrance while a group of us waited for our rideshare to take us across town. A friend and I intervened, somewhat cantankerously, and all three of us were cuffed and processed on some catch-all charge.

The incident stirred up enough controversy in our film circles that the organizers relocated the festival to a new city the next year (as if the police in this new city would react any differently).

In the holding cell, waiting for our respective producers, agents, and collaborators to post bail, the older filmmaker turned to us.

"That was some reckless shit. He was only going to ticket me. The next time you want to play Superman, go to a comic book convention."

~

I heard a tapping, light enough to pass unnoticed. I rose from the mattress and held my ear to the wall. The rhythmic patter left me to doubt my original suspicion of natural causes (the settling of pipes perhaps). Olivier Messiaen, when confined to a military prison during the Second World War, listened to the trills and whistles of birds. His chamber piece, *Quartet for the End of Time*, which was written in a detention camp and first performed by fellow prisoners, incorporated the sounds of the birds. The artist Tehching Hsieh made internment his medium, isolating himself in a wooden cage for an entire year. But unlike Messiaen or Hsieh, I felt no artistic impulse, no flight of inspiration, in this hard-hearted place. I kept my ear pressed against the wall for what seemed like hours. Evening emptied into night. I cleaved to the tapping sound as if it were a rain cloud in an otherwise barren desert. And then it stopped, with no explanation or forewarning. The following morning I listened again for the sound but heard nothing.

"Now that you've had time to rest," the inquisitor said. "I anticipate a more spirited conversation."

The room was arranged similarly, perhaps the same, as the first interrogation. However, on this occasion, the guard stood inside the door, his feet apart, hands held dutifully behind his back.

The man skimmed a small booklet in his lap, flipping pages in an idle fashion as if some mildly diverting magazine he picked up in a waiting room.

"Quite the traveler," he remarked. At this point I understood the booklet was my passport.

"What brought you to Bangladesh?" he asked, annunciating each syllable in the country's name.

"I was shooting footage for a documentary on the genocide during the Liberation War."

"And Burundi?"

"A film that never came together."

He made no acknowledgment of the comment. Was he waiting for me to provide a logline of the aborted project? Production notes?

"Did you friend Ali accompany you on these journeys?"

The mention of Ali's name blindsided me. I wondered

how long he had been harboring it in his back pocket.

"Ali is a common name."

"Lie if you must, but don't feign ignorance. We know of your relationship with Ali Jameel and the writer Sunni Salahi. According to our records, you met for breakfast at the restaurant in your hotel at 10:02 a.m. and departed at 11:23 a.m. Do I have that correct?"

I didn't respond.

"Mr. Rai, please attempt to be more cooperative. We have other forms of inquiry, if that is how you wish to proceed. But I wouldn't recommend it."

The guard behind him relaxed his hands, recoupled them in front of his body.

"We understand the inclination toward silence, but it may soon become tiresome."

"At least tell me what I'm being accused of."

He slid his pen into the binding of his notebook and folded over the cover.

"Espionage, my dear boy."

~

The illness started that evening. A creeping cold that sent my body into wild tremors. I crawled underneath the

39

mounded blankets on the mattress, my muscles struggling to fulfill even the simplest of commands. There was a painful tension in my forehead and in the bottom of my throat. I needed water, a small pill to mitigate the symptoms, but couldn't will myself to the door. The simple act of swallowing food seemed a monumental task. As night fell, a burning began in the palms of my hands, radiating across my body. A scorched earth campaign. I imagined being buried under a mountain of hot stones, trapped beneath an immovable weight that I couldn't free myself from. Sweat pooled in my jumpsuit, impressing on my mattress the outline of a body.

~

When I was twelve I was pressured into stealing cough syrup from a family pharmacy. The two boys I was with were older, steadfast, and practiced in the ways of petty theft. (When you're the only brown kid in your public school, you find ways to compensate for your outsider status.) While the older boys distracted the clerk, I weighted down my pockets with purple bottles. At the moment of truth, I lost my patience and bounded for the automatic doors, failing to grant them enough time to part. The glass doors knocked me backwards, and I fractured my arm in two places. My parents were called. They drove to the pharmacy to take me to the hospital. No mention was made of the indiscretion. In the car, my mother wrapped me in her arms, as if shielding me from an external force that intended to do me further harm. In my memory she only let go when I was returned to bed, a plaster cast encasing my arm.

~

The fever broke in the morning. With its coda came the rushing return of clarity. I consumed my breakfast—a pale lentil soup—with ravenous hunger. I asked the guard for new blankets and sheets. It wasn't clear whether he understood my request (or if he did, whether he would comply). I considered with a clear head my earlier conversation with the interrogator. Could my own carelessness have compromised the safety of Ali, of Sunni, of the members of SILO? What if the tapping I heard earlier was a coded message from an acquaintance, one I had recklessly imperiled in my pursuit of a story? On the other hand, could one of them have betrayed my name to save their own skin? A bargaining chip of little consequence. Either scenario seemed equally plausible and implausible. I put the questions out of my head, lest they smother me under their collective weight.

Two guards stood on either side of the door. They instructed me to collect my linens. I submitted without hesitation. They led me down the corridor—the opposite direction of the interrogation room (but, then again, all the hallways looked more or less the same). We took the staircase down two flights. A third guard met us at the landing and took charge of the company. The back of his uniform was untucked, but I made no mention of this.

He opened the door to a cell and the other guards shepherded me inside. The room was the same size as my previous dwelling, with three single beds crowded together: two stacked and one perpendicular. An older man with a mussed gray beard lay on the top bunk, his naked ankles crossed and hands behind his head. Below, a slightly younger man with a knit beanie perched at the edge of his bed, his leg trembling. The guards instructed me to deposit my linens on the unclaimed bed. They then exited the cell. An uncomfortable silence fell over the room.

"Welcome to the abyss," the older man called down.

After allowing me several minutes to settle, to take in my new living quarters, the men introduced themselves: Aasim and Naveed. Aasim, the older man on the top bunk, and Naveed, the younger, more serious one. They were university professors who taught at rival schools, but the competition seemed immaterial at this point.

"I wrote a paper for a European journal on Antonio Gramsci's conception of hegemony. It wasn't a major periodical. Just a small journal read by other academics in the field. After the publication, they broke into my house and arrested me—in front of my wife and daughter," Naveed said. "I can only imagine how terrifying it was for them to witness. The look on my daughter's face is something I will never forget."

"Me, I've never shied away from sharing my politics with my students. It was destined to catch up with me sooner or later," Aasim said, almost blissfully.

Naveed shot him a look of admonishment. Aasim turned to me and nodded, encouraging me to share my own story of internment.

"What is there to say? I wanted to shoot a film about the uprisings. I was careless, naïve. I believed my American passport would protect me from a place like this."

"Classic Yank," Aasim grinned. "You always think you can intervene in the affairs of others without consequences. But there are always consequences. In this country, only the very wealthy have impunity."

Naveed moved to speak but instead said nothing.

"How long have you been here?"

"Months," Aasim said "I may be a mathematician, but I've never been one for counting the hours."

"At this point either a family member pays an official for your release or you wait, sometimes for months, sometimes for years," Naveed said wearily, sliding his feet into slippers at the foot of the bunk and striding over to the elevated window.

"Don't worry," Aasim said. "Your people probably have helicopters over us right now, ready to blow a hole through the wall, and fly you out of here."

He made the whooshing noise of a helicopter out of the side of his mouth and lay back in his bunk, covering his face with a pillow.

~

Back in the interrogation room the inquisitor stirred his coffee cup with an outstretched finger. The lights were lowered to a less abrasive wattage.

"How do you find your new accommodations?"

"Cramped."

"I hope you've had time to think about our last conversation. I certainly don't want to make this more difficult than it needs to be. I expect your wife and mother would feel the same."

He set his coffee aside and tidied his papers.

"What did you and Ali Jameel discuss on August the seventh?"

"Science fiction novels."

The interviewer gave a curt smile. The guard rushed forward and cuffed the side of my head. The gold band around his finger caught the skin above my ear. Blood spilled from the wound as I pressed my hand against my head, believing that the pressure alone could staunch the bleeding. I cursed under my breath, leaning forward in the chair. The guard retreated to his post. The inquisitor crossed his legs.

"Care to try again?"

Aasim tore a thin strip of his bedsheet and helped me dress the wound.

45

"Each scar is a story," he murmured, stirring his hands around my head and securing the bandage with the knot.

"Not always one with a happy ending," I said. The wound still throbbed and my sight dipped in and out of focus. I wondered if I had a concussion.

"Chin up. The last thing Mohadessi's people want is an international conflict. You'll be out of here soon enough," he said. "Sooner than the rest of us anyway."

Naveed rose from his bunk. He paced across the small room. The frustration on his face was apparent.

"Don't cosset him," he said. "He returns home and— what?—writes a book, makes a movie, accepts a teaching post at a famed university. This is simply a footnote in his life. We will suffer the repercussions of this for years. Even if I'm let out, I will constantly be checking over my shoulder. I have to worry about my children and wife, whether they are safe. Who knows if I will even be able to teach again, if I can travel abroad again. There is no reprieve coming for us."

"Such a worrywart," Aasim said, dismissing Naveed's grievance with the flick of his hand.

Once every several days, at seemingly random intervals, a small caravan of prisoners would be led to the showers. An armed guard stood outside each of the eight stalls, checking and rechecking the identical watches on their wrists. The showers were repellant. The grout was yellowing and chiseled away. Hairline cracks spidered across the blue ceramic tiles. There was no shower curtain to cloister the prim or pious. The showerhead, brown with rust, delivered its water in spits and dribbles.

"One minute," the guard announced.

Ten seconds later: "Thirty seconds."

Before my body could acclimate to the cold water a hand took hold of my arm and hauled me out of the stall. The remaining shaving of soap slipped from my hand and circled toward the grumbling drain.

Aasim had proposed to teach me conversational Arabic: an offer I readily accepted. He seemed to derive joy from small acts of service, from imparting the obscure knowledge he had accumulated over the years. He used the cell as an oversized chalkboard, scratching characters onto the walls. Naveed watched our sessions with mild curiosity, sometimes interjecting to correct my syntax or pronunciations.

My tongue took to Arabic as if it were an ill-fitting suit, but when you have so little to occupy your mind, the rudiments of a new language much more easily take root. After only a few weeks of daily lessons, I was able to understand and converse freely in the local dialect—with only minor blunders to expose my lack of experience.

~

The lawyer wore an espresso brown jacket over a creased white shirt. His beard was finely trimmed and hair fastidiously combed to one side. He guided a miniature lint roller over his pant leg and then slipped it into his pocket. When I asked for a card, he responded curtly to the request.

"No card," he said, as if admonishing a small child for grasping for candy at a store checkout.

I took a seat across from him.

"I was sent by your people."

Who were my people? I wondered. The Americans, the Sikhs, the Brooklynites, the Directors Guild...

He had a briefcase laid out on the table and two

documents in front of him. His elbows were propped on the table and hands draped over one another.

"This is no place for you," he said. "I can make a request for your release, but I need your signature."

He pushed one of the two papers forward and handed me an expensive fountain pen. I read over the document slowly.

"This is a confession," I said. "I'm admitting to conspiring with the United States to overthrow the government."

"Is this not the truth?"

"I don't work for any intelligence agency."

"I can't help without your signature. You must make a confession, otherwise they will hold you indefinitely."

"I'm not confessing to a false charge. If I sign this, they will hang me."

He shook his head forcefully.

"You misunderstand," he said.

"This," I said, holding the paper up to his impassive face, "is a death sentence."

He seized the document and returned it and its companion to his briefcase.

"I offer my help, Mr. Rai. These are my conditions. Without your cooperation, then there is nothing I can do for you."

The gold latches on his briefcase snapped shut and he left the room.

~

"Do you know the Ship of Theseus?" Aasim said. He was snipping stray coils of hair from his beard. A guard stood inside the door, unwilling to let the pair of scissors out of his sight. Naveed was resting, so the question could only have been directed at me.

"I'm not familiar"

"It's a thought experiment proposed by Plutarch. He asked whether a ship would be fundamentally the same vessel if each of its planks were replaced with new timber."

"Or would it be a different ship?"

"Yes, precisely."

Aasim combed a hand through his beard, drawing out the loose hairs. The guard shifted uncomfortably.

"I used to believe it would be a new ship. After all, if none of the original parts remain, how does it retain its identity? But then I look at this government, this country. So much changes and yet so little changes. Different parts, same ship."

He turned to the waiting guard.

"How do I look?"

The guard opened his mouth to speak, changed his mind, and retrieved the scissors from the edge of the sink.

~

Aasim and Naveed were asleep in their stacked beds. I was struck by how effortlessly they slept under the circumstances. (Then again, only in sleep were any of us free.) Both men snored at a volume that bordered on the brash. The nasal sounds played less like a prepared duet than competing arias, an octave apart and out of key.

I used Aasim's contraband pencil, worn to the length of a golf pencil, to compose a letter that would never be delivered. I wrote an apology to Sanne—or rather a litany of apologies—for items as slight and commonplace as leaving the tube of toothpaste uncapped and hanging my jackets on the shoulders of chairs (and not in the dedicated coat closet). The exercise was an unburdening: each apology shifting the weight of gravity, bringing about a lightness of spirit. These were small hostilities that ruptured the ice over a deeper sea of discontent. Reconciliation wasn't in the cards, but maybe—with time—a kind of absolution. Naveed stirred in his sleep, moving me to stillness. The moon washed the room in a grim light. Once he settled and the snoring resumed, I lifted the pencil and continued my confessions.

~

The inquisitor shifted his chair forward, a few feet from my seated form, within the sphere of light. The face that had been concealed from me came startlingly into focus. There was a bluntness to his features, as if all the sharp edges had been sanded down for safe handling. I noticed his left ear was missing its lobe. His aftershave was overbearing from the diminished distance.

"Perhaps we should begin with a new question," he said, sitting upright in his chair. There was no folder or passport on his lap. "How is it that your travels brought you here?"

"I was not aware it was a criminal act to enter your country."

"The crime isn't entering, Mr. Rai. We welcome outsiders. The crime is consorting with state terrorists."

"You seem to be using terrorist rather loosely," I countered.

"Those who threaten President Mohadessi and our republic are most certainly agents of terror."

"I have conspired with no one."

"Why do you insist on lying? Do you wish to waste away here, to never see your wife again?"

"I have nothing to share."

"You're protecting people who would betray you at the first opportunity. What have they done to earn your silence?"

He stood and turned his back to me. The guard stepped forward.

"I am not your adversary, but if that is the role you wish for me, so be it," he said, and signaled to the guard, who slapped me across the face with the backside of his hand. The sound reverberated through the small room. My skin prickled, flushed red. He reached his hand back and struck again.

The inquisitor crouched and met me at eye level.

"What agency are you working for?"

The guard stepped behind me.

He guided his hands around my neck and pressed his index and middle fingers into the ridge of my windpipe. The flow of air thinned. Pressure built behind my eyes, and spots formed in my field of vision. I tried to speak but could only produce garbled sounds. He loosened his grip and then grabbed the back of my chair and dragged me across the concrete floor, the chair groaning underneath my weight.

The inquisitor opened a heavy door behind me, one I had failed to notice, and the two lifted me by either arm. Inside the concrete room was a bed frame. The frame was rusted with loose coils bent and disfigured. The guard held me down with his forearm and strapped my hands and ankles to the outer frame. The sharpened springs pushed through my shirt and dug into my skin. I tried to arch my back but was too weak to hold the position for longer than a few seconds.

"Mouth open," the inquisitor said. When I refused, the guard forced open my mouth with his hands and squeezed a wooden dowel between my cheeks. He proceeded to wrap a thin towel around my head, so I was unable to spit out the object. Each time I thrashed the springs sunk deeper into my back.

I heard the sound of a running faucet, the water hitting the bottom of a hollow container. The guard lugged over a plastic jug and began pouring it, slowly, over my head. Water filled my nose and mouth. The towel grew heavy and my breathing became labored. I coughed, tried to expel the water from my lungs.

"Too cold?"

I struggled to loose myself from the bed frame. (How was I supposed to talk when they were suffocating me?) The container emptied. The guard unfurled the towel and removed the straps from my limbs. My body rolled from the bed frame. I vomited the excess water and began gasping desperately, greedily, at the air. The inquisitor was speaking but I couldn't hear him. The gray room darkened and I collapsed to the floor.

~

When I recovered consciousness, I was supine on my bed, dirtied sheets curdled beneath me. I touched my neck and face; both revealed the onset of bruising. I contorted my head, looked across from me. Naveed was sitting at the edge of his bed, absorbed in a trance-like state.

"They took him," he said.

I glanced up. The top bunk was empty.

"Where did they take him?"

"I don't know," Naveed sighed. I turned onto my side. Above us, a moth thrashed its wings against the window, trying obstinately to cross the threshold of glass.

~

Through brief exchanges in the showers, word surfaced that protests at the local university had evolved into full-fledged rioting. Several protestors had been shot and killed. The rest were being rounded up and shipped to the prison. They were weeding the population to make room. Detainees were either having their sentences commuted or their execution orders expedited. There was still no news of Aasim or his whereabouts.

The uncertainty turned Naveed into a font of nervous energy. He couldn't remain still for more than a few minutes at a time. He responded distantly to inquiries, his reactions delayed or absent altogether. He ate only one or two bites of food, sometimes less, before surrendering his spoon. At night I heard him turning in his bed, uttering inscrutable words under his breath.

Two dour boys joined our company. They spoke sparingly and only to each other. I commuted to the top bunk. The boys rationed sleep on the single bed. One slept while the other rested fitfully on the concrete floor. A chivalrous impulse nearly persuaded me to resign my bunk, take solace on the cold concrete, but the urge passed. This was no place for petty heroics.

~

After a breakfast of stale bread and potato soup, the prison guards collected me from the cell. Naveed observed with silent resignation. Once the door was sealed, a hood was slipped indifferently over my head and a zip tie secured around my wrists. I was led down the corridor, a firm hand at my back. The guards led me down a set of staircases. I waited for a report from my dutiful minders, the mention of a destination. The longer we walked the more apprehensive I felt. A door buzzed, unlatched itself, and we entered into another part of the prison. I heard additional feet join the procession. I tried to estimate the number of escorts based on footfalls, but the mental math proved unreliable.

A stubborn door was uncoupled from its frame (after several forceful attempts) and a warm wind accosted us. I could feel the heat of the sunlight through the hood. My movements became heavy and labored. If this was the end of the line, I expected the courtesy of a phone call, or—despite having weened myself off tobacco a decade earlier—a cigarette. The guards halted in unison and marched back to the prison. The door closed behind them. Someone seized my arm and shepherded me into an idling car. The leather seats smelled newly upholstered. If anyone was seated next to me, or across from me, I couldn't sense their presence. The car advanced forward. Air conditioning coursed through the car, drying the sweat along the seams of my jumpsuit. I debated whether or not to speak, to cast my voice into the leathery void. I thought of my first visit to the country, several years earlier, and how I considered the appeals for caution and discretion overstated, born out of prejudicial fears of the unknown. But now I recognized that my cavalier attitude was the product of a different kind of privilege.

After thirty or forty minutes, the car came to a rest. The door opened and an outstretched arm hauled me from the car. I could hear the clash of traffic nearby, no more than a block away. (If I shouted, would someone hear me?) My escort guided me through another door. Sounds of the urban landscape were usurped by the orchestration of a commercial kitchen. Steel pans clattered and pots seethed. Commands in Arabic were lobbed across the kitchen, with no apparent concern for my forced passage. I could smell roasting lamb and my stomach shuddered with hunger.

I was led out of the kitchen and into a waiting elevator. The machine rose swiftly, elegantly, without betraying any sound of movement. The bell sounded and the doors slid aside. We walked down a hallway, heavy with the scent of cheap drugstore cologne. My handler knocked on a door. It opened almost immediately. Without a word I was funneled inside and placed in a stiff-backed chair. The hood was lifted from my head. Light poured in from the far window, and it took several moments for my eyes to adjust to their surroundings. Across from me sat Mohammad Mohadessi in a blue seersucker suit, a tuft of pink fabric peeking out of his pocket. His hair, striated with gray, was combed to one side. An elliptical beard framed his mouth. His eyes were small and embedded deeply in his stony face. I felt grossly underdressed for the occasion.

"How do you do, Mr. Rai," he said, his voice earnest and confident.

I struggled to manufacture the appropriate response.

"Fine."

"You must be famished."

A young porter in green livery laid in front of me a plate of roasted lamb, seasoned rice, and an imported beer with an accompanying glass.

"Eat," Mohadessi said. "Don't mind me."

I began to eat, abandoning any semblance of etiquette.

"You must be curious to know why you are here. As I understand it, you were mixed up in some unpleasant business. Fortunately, that is all over now."

A pair of formidable figures stood sentry on either side of the couch. A third person presided over my chair. I had paid little attention to them until now.

"You are a filmmaker of some renown."

"I suppose so. In certain circles."

"How would you like a special assignment?" he asked.

I didn't respond. I noticed my plate was empty, save for a few spared grains of rice.

"I wish for you to make a film about me and my work. Our country is, in some ways, set apart from the global community. It's important that they see what we are accomplishing here."

"I don't have any equipment."

Mohadessi waved his hand in a dismissive fashion. "Supplies we can get you. Whatever you require."

The liveried porter removed my plate and glass with a trained efficiency.

"Do I have a choice in the matter?" I asked.

Mohadessi laughed.

"Son, you always have a choice. However, different choices bear different outcomes. I say this not to perturb you. But if you are unable to perform this favor for me, then what use do I possibly have for you?"

~

Mohadessi's chauffeur turned down a private, cypress-lined drive. At the gate a military officer in a brown beret swept a bomb detector underneath the car, as if vacuuming beneath a bed. He nodded to his colleague in the security booth and the gates cautiously withdrew. The car circled a roundabout and came to a pause. I stepped out of the car. A tiered foundation sputtered at the heart of the roundabout.

The house rose three stories, formed from blocks of weathered sandstone, and spanned the length of a soccer pitch. Two marble lions stood guard at the front entrance.

I followed the retinue of security through the door. Inside, a grand staircase greeted us, fortified by floors of polished marble. An aging man as thin as a broom waited at the foot of the staircase.

"Chadli will show you to your room." Mohadessi said. He disappeared with his entourage down a side corridor.

Chadli led me upstairs. He was frugal in both speech and movement. We passed seven rooms before he unlocked a door and beckoned me inside. The dark marble floors were dressed with matching Persian rugs. There was a four-poster bed with folded linens atop a bloated comforter, a dresser and mirror, well-apportioned closet, and French doors leading to a small private balcony. Chadli showed me the attendant bathroom with its gilded fixtures, copper soaking tub, and heated floors. (Discrete temperature controls seemed to me the superior expression of luxury.)

He gestured to an intercom system beside the bed. "You need anything, press this," he said in his truncated tongue.

"What do I do about clothing?" I said, ill at ease in my prison fatigues.

Chadli walked over to the closet and tugged open the doors. An array of tailored suits, shirts, pants, and shoes revealed themselves, enough to dress ten men. They were arranged by color and function. He nodded in deference, and exited the room, leaving the door the slightest bit ajar.

~

There was a pleasant confusion to waking in an unfamiliar room: the self in isolate, removed from any kind of familiar context. A moment of pure consciousness before memory restores you to your rightful place in time and space. The windows, east facing, steeped the room in a wine-colored light. I rose from bed and stepped into the bathroom, relishing the extravagance of urinating without supervision or prying eyes.

I followed the staircase to the foyer, and from the foyer I navigated my way to the kitchen. Several cooks prepped breakfast, revolving around the open kitchen with feverish intensity. I sat down before a bowl of pitted green olives. Outside, through the glass doors, Mohadessi sat with several men in suits (none of whom I recognized), sipping a cup of coffee. One of the cooks set down two plates. One plate featured a short stack of unleavened bread, warm to the touch. The other bore a softened goat cheese, drizzled with olive oil, and orange jam. A copper carafe of coffee was poured from a precipitous height to cool the liquid, and the resulting cup was offered to me.

"Who is Mohadessi meeting with?" I asked.

The cooks didn't respond. They continued with their responsibilities undisturbed.

Two men of imposing stature joined me at the counter. Both I remembered from the hotel suite. We exchanged simple greetings. They didn't hesitate to begin furnishing their plates with spreads and assorted accompaniments.

"Shouldn't you be out there with the president?" I said and gestured outside.

"Shouldn't you mind your own business?" the larger of the two men said, taking such a rapacious bite of bread that the jam and goat cheese oozed out the side.

~

The day passed in an unresolved limbo. I didn't know which spaces I was welcome to and which were off limits, who I was permitted to address and who shouldn't be approached at all. Armed guards were posted around the house, wandering in the lackadaisical fashion of museum security. But none seemed especially concerned with my comings and goings.

I reclined by the pool, translucent blue, and browsed the

illustrations from a copy of *One Thousand and One Nights* that I found in Mohadessi's library. On the horizon, the sun began its slow decline. The wind passed at intervals, an antidote to the searing heat. I heard footsteps nearby and noticed a woman approaching. She moved with a cool assurance. Similar to the others in the house, her manner of dress was unmistakably Western: slim jeans and a buttoned oxford. The black headscarf was the only indicator of a cultural provenance. She assumed the lounge chair next to me. Up close I noticed the particulars of age: the faint imprint of wrinkles around her eyes and the liver line punctuating her forehead. She waited several moments before addressing me.

"And who might you be?" she said. "I know most of the faces around here. But I have never seen yours before."

"Vasant Rai."

"Pleased to make your acquaintance, Mr. Rai. And what might I ask brings you here?"

"Ignorance," I said, and then shifted the course of the exchange. "It seems I'm directing a film about President Mohadessi."

"I take it you have little choice in the matter."

I managed a weak smile.

"Here we have little control over our circumstances. Where you come from there is at least the illusion of choice."

"It's possible the illusion is better than the real thing. What, after all, is more oppressive than choice?"

"If I find out one day, I will let you know."

I raised my hand to protect my eyes from the waning sun. The woman slipped on a pair of tortoise shell sunglasses.

"I was told once that people who regain their hearing later in life are surprised to learn that the sun makes no noise."

"You're an odd sort, aren't you?"

"It permeates everything we see, without a sound. That's quite a feat."

"I suppose you're right."

"If you don't mind me asking, what's your name?" I said.

"Zahra," she said.

"And you work for the President?"

"In a manner of speaking. Mohammed Mohadessi is my husband."

My body became rigid as she disclosed this detail. I shouldn't have assumed a sympathetic ear.

"I apologize if I came off as discourteous in any way. I wasn't aware that the President was your husband."

"No need to censor yourself around me. I know what my husband is like. Nothing you can say will surprise or offend me."

"Can I ask why I'm allowed to roam freely? No one seems to be paying me any attention."

"Do you wish to have attention paid to you?"

"Not particularly."

"You are a guest of my husband, not a captive," she said. "You're welcome to any part of the house and grounds. Take a dive in the pool if you like."

I nodded in gratitude. This information was the closest thing I had received to an orientation.

"We start filming soon. Do you have any tips for lighting or shooting him?"

"Aim for the heart and don't miss."

~

Dinner was served outside, under the covered terrace. Mohadessi's personal chef, in his starched white uniform, sleeves meticulously folded, served braised chicken and rice, with a lightly dressed salad of tomatoes and cucumbers on the side. Mohadessi sat at the head of the table. Zahra occupied the seat to his right. Across from her was a pale, diminutive man in rounded glasses. The remaining seats were claimed by members of his security detail, including the two men from the morning. A single candle at the center of the table buffeted in the wind, but the flame endured.

"Has everyone met Mr. Rai?" Mohadessi asked. Heads turned promptly toward me. "He is a directing a movie about my presidency."

"Comedy or tragedy?" Zahra said. Mohadessi didn't acknowledge her comment.

"Do you know Scorsese?" one of the guards asked, the weight of the name landing on the penultimate syllable.

"Unfortunately I don't," I said.

A silence stole over the table, so I continued, "My films tend to be smaller, no big stars or special effects. Shoestring budgets. Let's just say no one is raring to invite me to any glamorous Hollywood parties."

"We will change that," Mohadessi said. "Whatever you need for this movie, we will get it. By the time this is over, they will be speaking of you in the same breath as Mr. Scorsese."

I suppressed the urge to laugh at that implausible claim.

"Who in Hollywood have you met?" the guard now asked. I thought carefully for a moment.

"Frederick Wiseman, Charles Burnett, Barbara Kopple, Werner Herzog."

There was quiet at the table. No recognition of these filmmakers.

"I once sat across from Bruce Willis on a flight to New York."

67

The body man perked up. "What was he doing?"

"Reading a magazine. *Time* or *Newsweek*, I think."

"Does he look the same as he does in the movies?"

"Shorter than you would expect."

The guards exploded in laughter.

"Die Hard's not so tough then, is he?"

"You've made their week," Mohadessi said, swilling his glass of sparkling water with a smile.

"It doesn't take much. A night with one of their cousins would make their week," Zahra said. The guards ceased laughing, stared at her with open contempt.

Mohadessi exchanged a string of heated words with her in an Arabic dialect I couldn't follow. She rose, dropped her napkin on the plate, and left the table.

"I apologize for my wife." Mohadessi paused, considering how to proceed. "She is not herself of late."

The pale man at Mohadessi's side piped up. "Mr. Rai, please discuss any filmmaking plans with me in advance. President Mohadessi has a very demanding schedule."

"Demir," Mohadessi said, laying a hand on his shoulder. "There is time enough in the day for all of it. How can we have time if we don't make it?"

Demir looked petulantly at his half-finished plate, the flame of the candle reflected in the curve of his glasses.

After dinner I followed Mohadessi down to the cellar level. The staircase was concealed behind a bespoke doorway, carved to blend seamlessly with the crown molding. At the foot of the staircase, Mohadessi switched on the overhead lights. The scene was not what I was expecting. A red carpet stretched out before us. Famous artifacts from classic films were encased in glass vitrines. They stood on either side of the narrow hallway, on marble plinths with custom engraved plaques. I felt like a diner in a chintzy Hollywood restaurant, the kind designed for wide-eyed tourists. There was Peter Fonda's leather jacket from *Easy Rider*, a shooting script from *Scarface*, a prop gun from *Bonnie and Clyde*, the Maltese Falcon from *The Maltese Falcon*. The exhibits were periodically interrupted by dormitory-style bedrooms. Through an open door, I espied one of the guards reclining in bed in his undershirt, toggling with his phone. Mohadessi beckoned me over to what I imagined what his prized possession: Le Coeur de la Mer from *Titanic*. I feigned appreciation for the collectible. (Though, in truth, I would have been far more impressed with a memento from the actual sunken ship.)

"Some men collect art," said Mohadessi. "But I am not a grandiose person. I take pride in more modest pleasures."

He stopped in front of a thick padded door. Mohadessi unlocked it with a generic key and I followed behind him. Inside were several rows of bulky leather seats, carpeted walls, and a projector screen. I had been in private theatres before, but had never seen a screen this expansive, comparable to that of a commercial cinema.

"My favorite room in the house," he said. He looked at me in search of confirmation of its opulence.

"It's quite a theatre," I said.

"Quite a theatre is right. This is where we'll be premiering the film once it's completed. Come and go as you please."

He handed me the key to the room.

"It comes with perks as well."

Mohadessi retrieved the remote from a concealed compartment by the door. He pointed it toward the waxen screen. The projector illuminated the room.

Julie Christie and Donald Sutherland were lying prostrate on the bed, leafing idly through a newspaper. I immediately recognized the scene from *Don't Look Back*. Christie began stroking the side of Donald Sutherland as the musical score crept in. Sutherland slid his head between her thighs, drawing open her robe with his hands. I remained fixated on the screen, stunned by what I was witnessing. Shots of Sutherland and Christie dressing interrupted images of the two tangled together in bed, leaving the viewer to wonder whether the sex was happening in that moment or if it was the recital of memory. When the scene finished, I turned to Mohadessi, who looked as though he had just devoured a satisfying meal.

Unable to sleep, I ran myself a hot bath. The copper tub turned the water a golden hue. I stepped into the tub and settled into the gilded water, the faucet still running. I considered the human cost of such luxury, the countless lives extinguished to furnish this home with Italian marble, crystal chandeliers, and semi-precious fixtures. (Not so different in a way from a conflict diamond.) In the course of my work, I had shared meals with perpetrators of atrocities, been welcomed into their homes and communities, but this represented a new form of complicity, of acquiescence to that which was ruthless and cruel. Here I was in Mohadessi's residence, bathing in this tub of tendon and bone. I walked barefoot on his heated floors, plucked books from his library, and slept underneath his high thread-count sheets. The water surrounding my body turned to lead. It darkened, became suffocating. Before the faucet had finished filling, I removed the stopper and drained the tub.

Demir decanted a silver kettle into two tulip-shaped glasses. He spooned a pair of sugar cubes into each glass, stirring with a monastic concentration.

"In Turkey, our tea is sacrosanct," he said. "The help doesn't know how to prepare Turkish tea—not correctly at least."

We convened in his office, which was secreted away in the very back of the house. We sat on opposing loveseats, a low table between us. I noticed Demir sat at the edge of the seat, his shoes barely reaching the floor.

"The president, for all his brilliance, is at times prone to flights of fancy. I feel a need to rein in your expectations. Mohadessi has commissioned artistic projects in the past, but he loses interest easily," he said, enunciating with a clear disdain the word *artistic*. "He is an uncommonly busy man with many curiosities."

"Does this mean there won't be a film?" I said.

"No, there will be a film. Whether there will be an ending to the film, that is a question I cannot answer," he said.

I finished my cup of tea and set it down on the table. Demir placed a coaster underneath the cup.

"I imagine you'll need equipment to make the film. Cameras and such?" he said.

"Those would be helpful."

He slid across the table a piece of stationery: "Write down what you need and we will secure it for you.'

I began preparing a list, circling back to cross out the more gratuitous and impractical requests. (As a colleague once told me, "If you ask for the moon, they will expect the stars.") I wondered how they would obtain the supplies, some of which were manufactured in countries imposing trade sanctions. I gave a final once-over to the extemporaneous list and returned it to Demir.

"To do this properly, I'll also need a crew."

"A crew?"

"A handful of workers to handle the equipment."

Demir furrowed his brow and tapped a finger against his pursed lips.

"This will not be a problem. Leave it to me," he said, rising from his seat, an indicator that our meeting had reached its conclusion.

~

I chanced upon Zahra in the library. She was curled in a red leather chair, a thin woven blanket over her lap.

"What are you reading?" I asked from the doorway, hesitant to enter without invitation.

"The poems of Emily Dickinson," she said. "I have a soft spot for English poets."

"She was American."

"That's a shame."

"I'm surprised the President collects so much Western literature."

"He collects everything," she said, nodding to the surrounding shelves without lifting her eyes from the page. "His collections fill the space where a personality is meant to reside."

I began to search the collection, as I had so often during my brief stay. The books were arranged by a system of Mohadessi's own design. For an outsider, the only way to browse was blindly.

"I take it you've read much of the collection."

"I have the luxury of free time."

"Do you ever watch films in the theatre downstairs?"

"That's Mohammad's space, not my own. Anyway, most movies put me to sleep. I appreciate that poems end before I can grow tired of them."

I nodded. I sensed I wasn't going to change her opinion on the virtues of film.

"How did you and the President meet?" I asked.

She looked up from her book, flustered for a fleeting moment.

"He was engaged to marry my sister. Before the wedding could take place, she was killed in a car accident." Zahra said, "I suppose I was cast in the role of her understudy. Though I was only fifteen at the time."

"That must have been difficult for you."

"It was a lifetime ago."

Moments later she rose from the chair and walked out of the library, departing without a word, presumably to find a quieter place to read.

~

Early in the morning, I swam several listless laps in the pool. When I returned to my room I discovered at the foot of the bed a stack of neatly packaged film equipment. A sticky note with my name was appended to the top-most package. I unboxed the contents: a digital video camera, tripod, shotgun microphone, boom pole, headset, crude lighting setup, a suite of pristine lenses (zoom, wide-angle, plus UV and neutral density filters), and a new laptop with an external hard drive. For a moment I forgot the assignment with which I'd been tasked, content to tinker with the equipment and take in its fresh out-of-the-box scent. Despite its questionable provenance, its impermanent nature, the tools of filmmaking never failed to draw me under their spell.

~

In Mohadessi's personal theatre, I watched Robert Bresson's *A Man Escaped*—a revelatory finding during my early film school days. Before Bresson, I didn't know you could make a thriller without actual thrills. He was a master of the slow unspooling of truths, each scene stretched to its breaking point. There was no great revelation or moment of release. Instead, tension was drawn out like a marble dancing along the edge of a table. Even the voiceover actor spoke in a tone bereft of emotion. Bresson sought authenticity in film, going so far as to hire non-professional actors. He wanted to strip cinema down to its elemental components. I yearned for this vision of authenticity, wanted it so much that I abandoned the imaginary world for the historical one, only to realize that what I thought of as *real* or *authentic* was just as rife with fiction and mythmaking.

As I passed the basement one of the bedrooms, I spotted Hasaam—the guard who had inquired about my industry connections—rolling up a prayer rug. I meant to move along, continue upstairs, but he noticed my presence through the open door.

"Yes?" he asked.

"I was looking for the horse head from *The Godfather.*"

His expression hardened.

"Please don't mock me," he said, taking my offhand quip for petty cruelty.

Stepping into the room, I steered the conversation to safer terrain. "How long have you worked for President Mohadessi?"

"Two—two and a half years," he said. "I was very fortunate to get the job. There is little work where I come from."

"And where is that?"

He smiled. "I could tell you, but you will not have heard of it."

"You're probably right."

I hesitated on whether to leave or linger. Hasaam continued, "The President has been very generous to me

77

and my family. I have money now to send home to my wife and daughter. It's not such a struggle anymore."

"And you like the work?"

"I am doing my service to the nation. At one time I wanted to work in the movies like you. Become a stuntman. But there is no movie industry to speak of—not here, not like where you come from."

"Bollywood isn't so far away."

"It's a long away from my family."

"At least I now know who to call if we need a stunt double."

He smiled sheepishly as he set his prayer rug upon the seat of a diminutive wooden chair.

"Not your friend Bruce Willis?"

"Too short."

~

Demir introduced the crew: a ragged and bewildered lineup of workers. They stood at stern attention, as if I were a drill sergeant preparing to bark orders.

"And they've worked on film sets before?" I asked.

"If they haven't, they will learn," Demir said. I took this response as a *no*.

I wanted to explain to him how challenging and time-intensive it would be to train a virgin crew, but I sensed he would dismiss this as a minor complaint.

I stood before one of the recruits. "Have you operated a camera before?"

"He doesn't speak English," Demir said.

"Marvelous."

"We can provide a translator if you don't feel confident in your own command of Arabic."

The crew began to squirm, shuffle their feet. Demir sent them away with the clap of his hands. They filed out of the room.

"I trust you have all you need to carry out the project," he said.

"We will see."

Demir nodded slowly. "Well, the time for requests is over. You begin filming tomorrow."

~

At eight in the morning, two black cars promptly pulled up to the house. Mohadessi entered the second car. I followed the crew and equipment to the first vehicle. Hasaam intercepted me en route to the back seat.

"The President requests your company," he said.

He walked me to the other car. Inside, Mohadessi sat

beside one of his security detail: a bald man with a thick, corded neck. (I later learned his name was Nasser.) I claimed the seat opposite them. The sky outside looked overcast through the heavily tinted glass.

Mohadessi studied my tired face.

"You don't seem excited," Mohadessi said.

"I'm carrying a lot in my mind."

"Are you someone who prays?"

"Not since I was a child," I said. My parents were lapsed Sikhs, quick to adopt the customs of their new country. We only went to temple as a matter of performance when distant relatives were in town.

"There is no shame in that. Children are the most pious among us."

The guard handed Mohadessi a thermos. He unsheathed the thermos and poured coffee into the adjoining cup. He blew on the steaming liquid before taking a sip, leaning over so the drink wouldn't dribble onto his impeccable suit.

"Is there a reason you never had children?" I said.

Mohadessi smiled impishly.

"That, Mr. Rai, is a very personal question. Let us say that political ambition and parentage do not always mix and leave it at that."

He continued, "I hope you will paint me favorably in this film of yours."

"I'm not so sure I have a choice in the matter."

Mohadessi finished his coffee and screwed the top back onto the body of the thermos.

"You are a difficult man to get to know," he said. "Some men are that way. I expect that once you see me among my people you will begin to warm up."

I turned to the window, watched the landscape pass in leaden tones.

~

Mohadessi exchanged handshakes with a series of older men in bespoke suits. Hasaam and Nasser stood at a measured distance. I checked the levels on the lavalier microphone clipped to his suit, made sure there was no outside interference. Two crew members assembled the camera and tripod as if they were unwieldy pieces of furniture. Short on patience, I stepped in and finished the task myself. Several domestic news outlets staked out positions on either side of us. Mohadessi nodded to one of the reporters. The man waved back, perhaps in too eager a manner.

A young woman in professional dress handed Mohadessi a comically large pair of scissors, while two men stretched a ribbon of red tape until it reached the length of the entryway. I focused the camera as Mohadessi prepared to make his remarks. He waited for the remaining reporters to arrange their microphones.

"My grandfather was a bricklayer. I knew him only briefly, but he was a man of sharp mind and strong constitution. On one occasion, he was hired to build a house of an unusual design for a wealthy architect and his new bride. My grandfather pointed out the flaws in the design, but the architect—who was educated and came from a better family than his own—insisted on the integrity of the blueprints. Mere months later, just as my grandfather had predicted, the house collapsed with the newlyweds inside," the President paused. There was a round of dutiful—albeit confused—applause. "I often imagine the monuments my grandfather could have built with the proper education, the right parentage. But we live in a changing time. I have no doubt the Muhammad Mohadessi School of Engineering will a set the standard for engineering universities and be the pride of our nation—and the envy of the West. Please join us in celebrating the opening of this peerless institution."

As Mohadessi drew open the mouth of the scissors, they broke into two equal halves. The university officials behind him looked momentarily panicked. The President cast the scissors aside and called over Nasser. The guard kneeled and withdrew a knife from the leather holster around his ankle. He handed it to Mohadessi. The President stepped forward and separated the thin barrier with a single stroke of the blade. The small audience—journalists included—broke out in rapturous applause.

~

I replayed the footage from earlier in the day. Beyond the sundering of the plus-size scissors, there was nothing remotely compelling about the captured video. It was bland hagiography: tedious and toothless in every way possible. Then again, why was I concerned with the quality of the final product? Who cared if the documentary was utter dross? Chances were Mohadessi would be perfectly pleased with shallow hero worship, a highlight reel of his executive exploits. Yet I continued to watch and rewatch the footage. No amount of reasoning could put me at ease, reverse the sense of anticlimax that came with creating something of so little merit.

~

Zahra was sweeping debris from the back patio. The house and grounds were emptied of their regular occupants.

"There's a groundskeeper for that, you know," I said.

She glanced up from her sweeping. "Idleness is just another name for sadness."

"So does that mean you never get sad?"

"It means I would rather sweep."

She paused and rested her chin on the end of the broom.

"Have you always asked so many questions?" she said.

"As far as I can recall. My mother would leave me in front of the television to keep me from prattling on," I said. "Then again, I suppose it's easier to ask questions than to answer them."

"And what questions will this film of yours ask?"

"I'm still working that out."

She hummed in acknowledgment of the response, a look of abstraction settling over her face, and resumed her tidying.

~

I was taught that a documentarian should always keep their subject at arms-length. Intimacy is the privilege of the viewer and the undoing of the filmmaker. For her graduate thesis, a college friend and classmate of mine went to live with the Quechua people in the Peruvian Andes. Two months later she had changed her name to "blessed one" in their native tongue and married a widowed alpaca breeder. Her family—heirs to a Connecticut pharmaceutical fortune—filed a sizable lawsuit against the school's arts department for indoctrinating their only daughter. The case was settled out of court for an undisclosed sum.

~

"I need access," I said to Mohadessi. This was my first view of his office, its shuttered blinds and mahogany surfaces. He leaned against the side of his desk. A bronzed bust of his head stood facing me. It felt like having a conversation with two people at once.

"What type of access?" he said, repeating the word with a well-founded suspicion.

"I can't make a film if you're cherry-picking moments for me to shoot. I need the freedom to decide for myself what deserves attention."

Mohadessi rubbed his chin and weighed the request.

"I admire your candidness," he said. "But I cannot afford to have camera people following me at every hour of the day. It would only serve as ammunition for my opponents."

"There won't be a crew. Just me. I'll be a fly on the wall."

"A fly on the wall?"

"You won't notice me. I'll stay in the background, out of sight."

"There are moments that cannot be recorded. I take my responsibilities seriously."

"Say the word and I'll turn off the camera."

The President hesitated before offering his hand. I seized it quickly and shook it.

~

The domestic staff and security populated the downstairs living room to watch a soccer match between their national team and a neighboring rival, a qualifier for a larger cup competition. They leaned forward in their seats as if their shoulders were burdened by an oppressive weight.

After a sliding tackle left an opposing player in a heap, the fullback was shown a yellow card.

"If we lose, it will be because of the official," Hasaam said. "He is a disgrace to the game."

"Clearly paid off," Nasser added.

Demir edged up beside me, slightly apart from the larger group. He gripped my arm and pulled me down to his humble height.

"The next time you want something from the President,

you come to me first," he hissed. "There is a chain of command. I trust that you can respect that."

On the counter attack following a turnover, the ball was crossed into the box and headed into the opponent's goal. The room erupted in euphoric celebration, startling in its intensity. Demir released my arm, thrust his fingers into his mouth and whistled, slipping seamlessly into the celebratory fervor.

~

Three men occupied Mohadessi's office: Demir, a military officer with a gleaming spectacle of medals, and another man of European persuasion. Mohadessi stood by his desk while the three men were seated, lending him the highest vantage point.

The officer doffed his cap and glanced at the camera lens with evident discomfort. He cleared his throat before he spoke.

"There are more protests at the university. We broke up a small gathering yesterday, but we lack the resources to maintain control and keep the instigators at bay."

"So what is your question then, Bilal?" Demir said critically.

"Do we have authority to use the necessary tactics to break up the protests?"

The European man sat with a sleepy languor, his legs crossed, and suit jacket crisply ironed.

"It's important to consider the optics of such escalation. The international community will respond if the actions intensify." His tone expressed a glaring lack of preference, as if he were simply playing devil's advocate.

"I've never let my judgement be clouded by the pieties of Western elites," Mohadessi said. He looked over at me, perhaps considering whether to ask me to turn off the camera. He elected to continue the exchange.

"These demonstrations are a threat to morale. Just because the protesters are students doesn't mean we can treat the situation lightly."

Demir nodded with vigor.

"Do you have a figure to propose?"

The General handed the President a folded sheet of paper. Mohadessi skimmed the request.

"Our petroleum exports are very strong right now. We don't want to jeopardize that with boycotts or tariffs," the European man said.

Mohadessi raised his hand to silence the group. His mind was made up.

"This is not enough. It's a pittance. We will double it."

"That is very wise, sir," Bilal said. The officer saluted the President and the three men exited the office. I kept my camera trained on Mohadessi. He turned suddenly to me. "You can turn that off now."

~

Most evenings, after dinner (and without waiting the recommended thirty minutes), I swam laps in the pool. It was all that could keep me from missing the familiar comforts of home. I wanted to call Sanne and hear her voice, which began to feel more like a phantasm, the residue of dreams. I didn't tally the laps as I swam or count the minutes I spent in the water. Instead, I finished when a deep aching pain traveled up my biceps and reached my shoulders. The water was illuminated by footlights on the pool floor. Every morning Mohadessi had the pool purged of every twig, weed, and insect. No speck of detritus escaped the cleaner's sight. A substandard athlete in school, I took to swimming as a physical outlet. Later, I began to think of the water as a bridge language, common to people in every geography, regardless of color or age or creed. It became the thing I did after long shoots in isolated places (shoots that kept me away from Sanne and other partners before her). I could release the frustrations of the day and settle my mind before the next skirmish with an overbearing producer. Tired and sated, I pulled myself onto the ledge of the pool. Water spilled down my hunched form. I held myself there, eyes sealed, breath heavy, until I was finally ready to return to the house.

~

Mohadessi sipped his cappuccino, his first two fingers curled around the porcelain handle. He looked over the crystalline pool, the auburn hills beyond, then turned to the camera, which was directed squarely at his face.

"And this is compelling cinema?" he asked quizzically.

"It's humanizing," I said, pausing the recording. "Most people in the country only see one side of you. Sometimes the most persuasive scenes happen when observing people in their private moments."

"I'm not sure why a human needs humanizing."

"You'll have to trust me on this."

He nodded slowly. "You are the professional, Mr. Scorsese. I won't interfere with your work, just as I wouldn't expect you to interfere with mine."

~

I read the first half of *Heart of Darkness*, cozied in one of the library's plush leather chairs. The copy was prehistoric and the pages when I turned them creaked and groaned, as if inconvenienced by my idle leafing. Chadli entered without the slightest sound. When I looked up, he was staring at me with a heavy-lidded expression.

"You have been invited to see an opera with Mr. and Mrs. Mohadessi," he said in his streamlined speech.

I was struck by the mention of Zahra as the wife of President Mohadessi, having not heard that honorific until that moment.

"Yes?" Chadli pressed. The task of extending the invitation seemed an undue burden, and in that moment he wanted nothing more than to bring this conversation to its terminus.

"Yes," I said. "I have no other plans as far as I know."

His face slackened with relief. He collected my teacup from the side table, still three-quarters full, and floated silently out of the room.

~

A tailor took my measurements after breakfast. When I returned to my room in the late afternoon, a tuxedo—jet black and ironed smooth—was draped over the edge of the bed. I appraised it. It fit like a second layer of skin. Accompanying the tuxedo was a pair of black shoes, polished to a mirror-like sheen, and a neatly folded bowtie.

In the car Mohadessi and Zahra sat far enough apart—their bodies angled away from one another—that they could have been strangers splitting a cab. Zahra wore an arresting maroon dress and over her head a white silk scarf. It was difficult not to stare.

Mohadessi tried to incite conversation.

"I hear you've been making good use of my library," he said.

"It's quite a collection," I said.

"As a younger man, I was rarely seen without the company of a book. But there are only so many hours in a day. I prefer to spend my spare time now in the company of friends and loved ones."

"I must have missed those younger days," Zahra said, the trace of a smirk on her face.

"There is much you don't know about me," he said.

"I'm sure that's true."

The statement of assent effectively ended the conversation. I closed my eyes and waited for the vehicle to reach its destination.

Stepping out of the car, Mohadessi and Zahra interlocked arms. I trailed behind them as they greeted society people and aspiring climbers. How effortlessly they slipped into their assigned social roles, letting the dramatics of earlier—their animosity toward one another—melt away.

Once inside, they separated. I circled the marbled atrium, pilfered a handful of shrimp from a revolving tray (no sign of cocktail sauce). The women clustered in one corner, while the men commandeered the center of the lobby, cleaved to caucuses that validated their class and social status. Mohadessi waved me over to an alcove by the staircase and introduced me to a handsome young man in a dark blue tuxedo.

"Amar is the finest actor of his generation," Mohadessi said, patting the thespian on the shoulder. We shook hands. "Mr. Rai is a celebrated Hollywood director. He is making a film about me."

"A director like Scorsese?"

Why did everyone insist on comparing me to Scorsese?

"I only shoot documentaries," I said, to his clear disappointment.

"You have never considered making an action film or drama?"

"I'm not sure it suits my strengths as a director."

"You and I may have to convince Mr. Rai otherwise. He would make an excellent action director," Mohadessi said, now with a hand on each of our shoulders.

I didn't want to explain to them how no producer in the right mind would entrust a multi-million dollar blockbuster to a career documentarian. I had a difficult enough time raising enough money to keep my crew members in accommodations with functioning plumbing. Most of the seed money for my projects came through grants or wealthy benefactors.

A warning issued from the announcement system. Zahra dutifully rejoined us, and I followed her, Mohadessi, and Hasaam up the staircase. The hem of her red dress swept across each step. We followed Mohadessi to a private box on the mezzanine level. The box was separated by burgundy curtains. I took a seat behind Mohadessi and Zahra.

My own relationship with opera was ambivalent at best. It neither pleased me nor agitated my nerves. As holders of season tickets, Sanne's parents had invited us to the opera on numerous occasions, and we were happy to oblige, but a deeper interest never took root. The medium lent itself too easily to melodrama for my own tastes.

The opera recalled Puccini, despite claiming to be an original work. I scanned the program for references. Mohadessi whispered to me about how in demand the librettist was in Europe.

I observed with an unsteady focus, my attention losing its foothold, and then it would be forcefully restored by a high-pitched note. The mistress of the sculptor flew into a jealous rage when she noticed his latest composition resembled another woman (her cousin, in fact). Just as she had seized the sculpture to shatter it, Zahra rose from her seat and withdrew from the balcony. Mohadessi, entranced, made no recognition of her egress. The bust splintered into hundreds of pieces and the sculptor dropped to his knees, bellowing with his hand stretched toward the wreckage.

I stood and quietly passed through the curtains. Hasaam remained stalwartly in place at the rear of the balcony. Zahra was resting against the wall, drying tears from her flushed face. She glanced at me, her reddened eyes pinched together.

"Have you ever been so trapped that you felt you were suffocating?"

I nodded gently.

"When I was in the prison."

"Of course," she said, ashamed at her question. "Sometimes the emotion overcomes me."

"It's fine. Human even."

She smiled weakly, the expression giving way to deeper grief. She closed her eyes and took a slow breath. I stepped toward her and placed my arms around her back. I felt her muscles soften. She rested her head on my shoulder. After several moments she looked up and uncoupled herself from me. Mohadessi was standing beside the red curtain, a twisted smile on his face.

"The act has finished," he said.

~

A car came for me the following afternoon. I made to retrieve the film equipment from its storage place.

"You won't need it," Hasaam said.

He led me outside into the stifling heat. I didn't know how he managed to bear it, in his pressed black suit and protective vest (the outline of which was unmistakable under his white shirt). There wasn't so much as a drop of sweat on him.

The ride was short, no more than three minutes, a distance that could have been traversed easily on foot. The driver let us out beside an overgrown patch of land. Mohadessi was there among a herd of grazing sheep, huddled in small masses. As I neared, I realized the support he was leaning on was a bow: hand-carved and chest high. The revelation momentarily slowed my approach, but Mohadessi spotted me and gestured me over. I stood beside him as he gauged the rounded target, which rose from a corner of the fencing, like a traffic sign designed for livestock.

"I used to shoot rifles," Mohadessi said. "But then I was introduced to archery."

He leaned the arrow against the frame, drew back the bowstring, and—after the slightest of hesitations— released his grip. The arrow struck the target with a dull thud, alighting just outside the innermost circle.

"Are you a sportsman, Mr. Rai?" he asked.

"I fear I lack the competitive instinct."

"I doubt that. One doesn't rise to the top of their field without some desire to surpass others."

He loaded the bow again and drew back the string, released. It landed inches from the first salvo.

"Firearms have existed for several hundred years, longer in the East. The bow, on the other hand, predates recorded history. It is native to us, its motion etched in our muscle memory—the same muscles that teach us to walk and breathe. There's something beautiful in that."

I saw Hasaam in the distance. He had separated from us at some point and was holding a lamb in his arms. The animal brayed but made no effort to escape. He laid the lamb down beside the target, harnessing it to the fence post so it couldn't escape. Mohadessi lifted his bow and fired, piercing the lamb above its shoulder joint. Its back legs gave out and it keeled over, without resistance or struggle.

"I hope you have an appetite. We will be eating well tonight," Mohadessi said.

Hasaam dragged the dying animal by its hind legs, leaving in its wake furrows of crushed grass.

"I don't understand why you brought me here," I said.

"Because a little bit of fresh air does a person good."

I nodded obligingly, though all I could smell was the scent of decay.

~

I sat in the back row of the theatre. It had started to feel like the only place in which I was truly alone—a refuge in an otherwise inhospitable space. I stared at the gray screen and imagined barricading myself in the tiny theatre, as Howard Hughes was said to have done: growing out his beard and nails, surviving on chocolate bars, urinating into milk bottles. How long would it take for them to notice I was gone? And how much longer before they were pounding at the door, demanding I let them in? Even though I knew I wouldn't risk it, there was a comfort in playing out fantasies of willful disobedience. My own mettle was missing in action, especially compared to the subjects of my films. I envied the courage of those who could navigate impossible circumstances, confront powerful people without blinking an eye. There was nothing like a suburban American upbringing to cultivate a cowardly condition.

~

Mohadessi swiveled impatiently in his office chair. I screwed the camera onto the tripod and began adjusting the reflectors to corner the remaining shafts of afternoon light.

"What is it you would like me to do?" he said.

"Respond to several questions. People will be interested to hear your thoughts on politics and leadership. I'd like these conversations to act as a tissue that bind the narrative together."

"Let me know when you'd like to begin."

"Just one more moment" I said.

Mohadessi made a gesture of bored acquiescence. I stood behind the camera and began recording.

"When did you decide that you wanted to go into politics?"

"The decision wasn't mine to make," Mohadessi said. "As of course you know, my father was a leader in the party. There was never any question that I would follow the same course. Here, in the East, we make career and family decisions as a collective, as those choices have an impact on the generations before and after us."

"What was your relationship with your father like?

"Difficult, at times. My father was not a kind or compassionate man. He did not forgive easily. That is the difference between us. I believe that corrupted men can redeem themselves. Though I have not always been proven right in this regard."

"Do you consider yourself a moral person?"

Mohadessi's lip curled into a rakish smile.

"Morality is in the eye of the beholder. You should understand this better than most, Mr. Rai. I do what is right for my country. Your leaders do what is right for yours. I am not naïve to how I am perceived abroad. The conflict arises when your country seeks to exercise its dominion over us in the name of morality. That is superiority, not morality."

"Some might question the morality of granting yourself a lifetime appointment."

"Who?"

"Some."

"Poor sports."

"You find nothing wrong with this kind of authority?"

"I've given us stability where there was none. The sudden changes in government have harmed our people and stood in the way of our progress. Now we can begin to move forward."

"Are you not fearful that one day people will seek to overthrow you?"

"Fear is a crippling emotion. Were I to preoccupy myself with every threat against me, I would never get anything accomplished. I have freed myself from fear—especially fears of my own mortality."

"There are what—twenty, thirty—guards around the grounds? Fear must play a role in that."

"I keep myself protected so our country does not descend into chaos."

"So you don't dismiss the idea that people may grow impatient with your leadership?"

Mohadessi rose from his chair and stared at his bookcase, his back turned to the camera.

"That is enough questions for one afternoon."

Zahra was sitting in my bedroom by the window, the blinds drawn so that no light escaped. She wore no head covering and her black hair ran freely down her shoulders.

"You shouldn't be here," I said.

"I shouldn't be here," she repeated as if lured into a spellbound state.

"Someone could have you seen you."

"I was careful. This was the only place that felt safe to go."

She fingered the folds of the curtains.

"This was once my room, some years ago, but I found the morning light too obtrusive," she said.

"I have a kinder opinion of light."

"My sister and I would imagine living in a house of this size, with gardens like the Palace at Versailles. She was fortunate in many ways—not to have those dreams of childhood punctured," she said. "A child cannot conceive that someone with everything can also have nothing."

"Would it be so hard to leave?"

"Easy to leave, harder to disappear. I surrendered fantasies of escape long ago."

Zahra moved to sit down on the bed, but thought better

of it, as though the threshold crossed would be one from which she could not return.

"I should go," she said. "Can you check the hallway?"

I opened the door a crack, enough room to peek my head through.

"All clear."

Zahra stepped past me, touching her hand to my upper arm, and slipped soundlessly out of the room.

~

A luncheon for business leaders was held in the ballroom of a ritzy downtown hotel. I filmed Mohadessi from the wings of the stage. He delivered a speech he had delivered dozens of times before. Names and platitudes were changed but the essence remained the same—a hearty cocktail of economic grandstanding and nationalist pride.

"Our country succeeds because it is built on a strong foundation. Without values, without reverence toward the Almighty, a nation will come undone. We see this every day in the West: lawlessness and hubris."

At moments of emphasis he brought his palm down on the podium, his gold ring lending added resonance.

While Mohadessi shook hands and made repetitive

conversation in the thinning ballroom, I retreated to a table in the back of the room.

A bearded man with an audacious gut assumed the seat next to me and proceeded to empty into his steaming cup six or seven packets of sugar.

"Sekhr Safar." He offered his hand before continuing. "I export textiles. Rugs and such," he added, in case the reference of textiles was insufficient.

"Vasant."

"Indian? Very interesting. And you work with President Mohadessi?"

"In a manner of speaking."

He sipped the coffee with two hands, almost protectively.

"May I speak openly with you, Vasant?"

I nodded.

"You see these people?" he said, motioning to the suited industrialists come to hand-deliver their blessings to Mohadessi. "Today they kiss the ring, tomorrow they come for blood. Most of us have lived through enough unrest to know when a storm is on the horizon. We can feel it in our bones."

He emptied another packet of sugar into his dwindling coffee cup. "I hope your President has packed an umbrella."

Hasaam supervised a convoy of workers as they ferried trunks and luggage to the front door. His eyes darted back and forth with a look of deep wariness.

"What's going on?" I asked.

"President Mohadessi wishes to go to the desert for the weekend," he said.

"The desert?"

He ignored my kneejerk question. His focus remained on the succession of porters, manifesting luggage from some unknowable recess of the house.

~

The helicopter lifted off shortly after the door was pulled shut and Demir—the final passenger—was seated beside me. Mohadessi sat across from us, flanked by Nasser and Hasaam. He tapped on his headset, signaling to me to don my own pair.

"Is this the first time you've traveled by helicopter?" he asked.

"No," I said plainly.

There were remote areas, unfrequented outposts of

civilization, inaccessible to commercial flights, and several times I had been forced to charter helicopters or private planes. Still, I'd failed to accustom myself to the deafening noise, which enveloped us in its aural cocoon.

"Let us know if you plan to be sick," he teased, sensing a rigidity that seemed at times my default setting.

I had no desire to make conversation with Mohadessi, Demir, or any of the passengers in the aircraft. Once we reached our cruising altitude, I switched off the headset radio and turned my eyes toward the window, the boundless blue that lay beyond.

~

At the camp young men in colored headscarves and white robes erected tents and canopies. The evening was dry and cool with a restless breeze that shaved furrows into the waves of sand. The sun, ruby-red, rested imperiously on the horizon. I walked past a one-armed man with a falcon perched on his surviving forearm, the bird strapped in a bejeweled mask. Behind him was an unsteady tower of caged birds, one stacked on top of the other. The birds, though varying in size, resembled one another in color: gray-flecked wings and bright yellow talons. They remained still and silent in their tailored masks, blind to the events happening around them. At the periphery of the camp, a dozen black Land Rovers were parked at a slight cant. Each was as immaculate as the next. Breaking with tradition, a white Rolls Royce pulled up alongside the matching vehicles. An elaborate hood ornament punctuated its presence. On closer inspection, I recognized it to be a live bird.

~

Mohadessi sat on a tufted pillow in a tangerine-colored robe. His tent rivaled the size of my Brooklyn apartment.

"Did they show you to your sleeping quarters?" he said.

"They did."

Earlier in the afternoon one of the attendants escorted me to a subdivided tent, generously proportioned, where my bags lay in wait.

"What's the reason for this trip?" I asked.

"Does there have to be a reason for everything?" Mohadessi said. "The weather was ideal for racing and there was nothing on my schedule that couldn't be moved to a later date."

"Be at ease, soldier," he said, making a calming motion with his hand. "This is meant to be a time of leisure."

Leisure. It was a curious choice of word to produce in front of someone being held against their will.

A boy chopped firewood lodged in a rubber tire. The desert scene felt out of a dream. He moved purposefully around the tire, bringing his ax down on the log until it had broken into even quadrants.

I stood closer to watch him. He took no notice of me. I wondered how a boy so young could muster the strength to split the wood.

In time, he introduced himself as Basheer and I asked questions of him out of curiosity. He said he lived in a village at the edge of the desert.

"I guide people. I carry trunks. I cook," he said. "Whatever they pay me to do."

"What about school?"

The boy laughed and brought down the ax on a new log. He struck me as a child wiser to the ways of the world, its requirements for survival, than most adult men.

I asked him if I could try my hand at chopping. He shrugged and handed me the blade. I examined it briefly, felt its weight in my palm. Then I drew it above my head and brought it down with full force. The heel of the ax embedded itself in the surface of the log. I tried to remove it but it wouldn't budge. The boy stepped around me, put his sandaled foot on the tire, and withdrew the ax without struggle or ceremony.

~

Dinner was cooked with great attention over an open flame. Squab, pierced with long skewers, were rotated at precise intervals. The men had broken off into smaller groups for socializing and games of cards. Flasks were exchanged, filled with foreign liquors strictly verboten by law. Demir stood at the edge of the flames, transfixed as I was, his hands clasped behind his back.

"I notice you didn't pray with the others," I said.

"I was raised in a secular household," he said. "Religion has never held sway over me."

"There are times when I wish I still had faith. It's possible I never had it, that I just took comfort in the rituals of the faithful. Though perhaps that is the same thing."

"One can have faith in things other than God," he said. Smoke rose from the birds, their crisping skin. "Fortunately, President Mohadessi appreciates the many forms that faith takes."

"And what do you have faith in?"

He turned solemnly to me. The flames in his glasses

109

were replaced with the cold desert landscape. "Money, Mr. Rai."

~

    These were only test runs, trials designed to show off the falcons to prospective buyers. The morning was warm and promised warmer. Most of us—thirty or forty people—took refuge under the shade of the canopy. The breeders exhibited the birds, their outspread wings and finely manicured beaks and talons, before slipping off their masks with a practiced delicacy and lifting them, one by one, into ecstatic flight. The birds broke free of their masters and beat their wings with great rapacity, aiming to make an impression. Motion sensors marked the start and finish of the course, and flight times were displayed on an electronic board held up by a young, turbaned man. I struggled to keep the falcons in the camera frame. I didn't want to resort to zooming out, relegating them to mere specks on the desert horizon. Onlookers referred to sheets that assigned a number to each falcon. They made notes in journals or on their phones, conferred in hushed whispers with one another. In the distance, several hundred meters out, a man swung a rope, baited with carrion. As the falcon neared, the offering was whipped away. The falcon lifted and turned, its wings at full and glorious stretch. For their exploits, the birds were treated to the leftover pigeon from the night before and sprayed down with cool water. I was struck by the novelty of the contest, which Mohadessi had ironically dubbed the "sport of princes." Victory was the product of neither rarefied talent nor the acquisition of a particular skill. It was achieved by pure submission, dominion over a wild creature whose nature was to hunt and kill.

~

In the waning hours of the evening, the men congregated in the main tent. The breeders offered up their birds. A bidding war erupted for the first entry, rocketing to over ninety thousand American dollars (if my amateur math was accurate). There was no hint of triumph in the face of the highest bidder. The transaction carried the kind of joy one might feel feeding loose coins into a parking meter. The other falcons—eleven, in total—went for sums ranging from forty thousand to eight-five thousand. The talons of the birds were tagged, announcing their new ownership, and then set aside in cages covered with faded cloth. The President bid on one of the last birds. His offer went unchallenged.

I went out to the boundaries of the camp to relieve myself. The temperature had dropped precipitously, and I aimed to finish my business in a swift fashion. Against the violet backdrop, I noticed a pair of lights approaching, the dull rattle of an engine. A white van came to a halt beside the other cars, about a hundred feet from where I stood. A hulking man in a gray suit stepped down from the cab and lifted his phone to his ear. Less than a minute later the prodigious spender who was outdueled for the first falcon (but went on to claim several others) exited the tent and greeted the man and his colleague in the passenger's seat. He pointed to an auxiliary tent behind the grand canopy. The large man opened the van door and out stepped four women, the first of whom embarked tentatively, as if the sand were the surface of a distant moon. They wore sheer kaftan dresses, embroidered with gold, leather sandals, and headscarves. I could tell by the way they held their bodies in the cold that these were not women, but rather young girls at the tail end of adolescence. They were led, bookended by the men, to the designated tent.

I began to feel nauseated, sick in a way I hadn't felt since my time in prison. The nausea rose in my throat and I expelled my dinner—its unflattering contents—onto the sand. When I looked up again, the women had disappeared into the tent. The engine of the van, sapped from its lengthy journey, sat there cackling.

~

While men of status sipped their morning tea, their hired hands packed up the camp, disassembling tents and beds and placing them in the backs of Land Rovers, or tying them down to roofs with braided rope. As efficiently and unceremoniously as it was erected, the camp was dismantled. The white van from the previous night was gone. I saw Hasaam and Nasser place Mohadessi's trunks in the back of one of the black SUVs. Soon it would transport us back to the helicopter and then to the house. The sand shifted and resettled beneath us, coaxed along by the wind. There would be no trace that we were ever here. The desert would erase us, wipe the slate clean.

A spindle of a boy carried a caged falcon away from his body, uncomfortable with handling the bird of prey. Some would be delivered to palatial homes, other collected on site. The lack of a marker indicated this bird was unclaimed, had failed to tease out a single bid. The falcon made a dim, searching noise. The boy set the cage in the back of a car—a model of unremarkable pedigree—and closed the door.

My mother held the unshakable belief that illness was as much a mark of spiritual imbalance as it was of a physical one. Proper restoration called for addressing both sides of the equation. For days I remained in bed. My body was drained of all its stamina, and it was a feat just to make it to the bathroom or closet. Sweat soaked through my sheets on more than one occasion. I would have to raise myself onto my forearms and crawl to the floor as I waited for one of the domestic staff to swap out the bedding. The fever gave way to bodily chills that bore deep into my bones. It was nearly a week before I summoned the strength to walk to the kitchen and slather a pat of butter on toast. I didn't see Mohadessi during this time. Or Zahra. Or Demir. And the only words I spoke were simple requests delivered in hoarse whispers. At night, stricken with feverish flights, I dreamed of complex labyrinths.

Hasaam sat on a stool facing the lens of my camera. I was experimenting with widening the breadth of the interviews to include those who knew Mohadessi most intimately.

"Try to relax," I said. His shoulders were rigid and arms resting unnaturally on his thighs. Nothing about his posture evinced comfort.

"We're just going to have a conversation," I said, adjusting the setup to better illuminate his face. He tried planting a second foot on the ground, and thinking better of it, returned it to the lower rung of the stool.

"Is it difficult living apart from your family?" I asked.

"Every day it is hard. But I have no choice in the matter. In a year, perhaps two, I will have enough money to buy a small property and bring them to the city to live," he said, considering each word carefully.

"Do you ever resent the fact that you can't have both—your job and your family nearby?"

"Resent?"

"Feel anger towards."

"I feel no anger. None. It is a part of Allah's plan. I am fortunate to have this job when so many are without one."

"What makes a man like Mohadessi worth sacrificing so much for?"

"Mohadessi has made our country strong again. He has brought back the rule of law. Before Mohadessi there was no hope, nothing to feel pride about. Now we have shopping centers and restaurants and new hotels. A movie industry," he said, indicating to me behind the camera. "There is

115

nothing I wouldn't sacrifice—not myself, not my wife, not my children—for President Mohadessi."

Hasaam folded his arms with an air of quiet triumph as if he had passed a test I had naively expected him to fail.

~

Still too weak to swim laps, I took a morning constitutional around the grounds. It was during one of these walks that I chanced upon Zahra, looking out absently over the rose gardens behind the house.

"I heard you were ill," she said.

"Nothing that can't be walked off."

She nodded and turned quiet.

"I'd like to interview those closest to Mohadessi for the film. Is there a time we can speak formally on camera?"

"I fear you may be taking my husband's project too seriously."

"I'm not sure I have the luxury of taking it unseriously."

"I have no desire to be in your film," she said with a finality.

"Is everything okay?"

The solicitous nature of my question seemed to rankle her.

"All is fine. It was fine before you arrived here. It will be fine once you are gone."

"Zahra."

"What is it in men, even the most powerless, that make them think they can fix things?"

She turned to face me straight on, awaiting a response to a question I had no answer for. A landscaper, farther down the lawn, paused his shearing and looked at us. Zahra shook her head dismissively and walked past me.

~

In the library, I browsed volumes of art books. Sometimes during shoots I turned to visual art for inspiration (or hopeful intervention). I paged through a copy of Hokusai's woodblock prints, still balancing on the step ladder. A slip of paper fell out of the book. I stepped down to retrieve it. It was a plane ticket. The printed destination was London Heathrow Airport. The ticket bore Zahra's name, and underneath a date and time that had long since passed. It seemed unlikely that this was a planned excursion, to which Zahra was seldom privy, and which wouldn't require hiding the ticket in such an inexplicable place. I considered then how little I knew about her, and whether what I did know was a projection, born of a need to fit her into a tidy box of my own making. Did she follow through with the trip or get cold feet? Had she been planning to meet someone on the other side? Or was there a far simpler and more mundane explanation? I wondered why she had chosen the book of Hokusai prints, a volume that demanded a ladder to reach. One fact I knew about Hokusai was that he was known by dozens of different pseudonyms throughout his career, changing his name to reflect shifts in his style. I slid the ticket into the binding and snapped the book shut. I returned the book to its lofty haunt.

~

Once I had packed the camera in its cushioned carrying case, Mohadessi rose from his office chair and leaned against the side of his mahogany desk, right hand stowed in his pocket.

We had just completed a short interview, no more than twenty or thirty minutes. The fragmented recordings lent Mohadessi a sense of control over the proceedings. There was no time for questions to veer into inhospitable terrain.

"I have heard you've been spending quite a bit of time with my wife," he said, flashing a gentle smile to preempt any defensiveness on my part.

"We occasionally chat in passing," I said.

"Take her words with a grain of salt. Her mind is not steady," he said, pausing. "She has not been right for a long time."

"I don't get that impression."

"I have flown in doctors from Switzerland. I have paid to send her to the best medical clinics. None of it has proven effective. The Zahra you know is not the woman I married."

"Perhaps you don't know the woman you married."

"You should measure your words more carefully, Mr. Rai."

"I will take that into consideration."

Another wry smile flickered across his face.

"For your sake I hope you do," he said.

~

The kitchen staff was huddled around a small television. Up until this point, the television had remained inanimate, and I had paid it little attention in its discreet recess. When I entered the kitchen, the staff shut off the power and circulated, drifting into the dining area to lay out place settings and silverware.

I switched on the television. On the screen, roiling masses swarmed the city's central square, raising flags of the opposition party and chanting impassioned demands.

Tanks and armored vehicles patrolled the boundaries of the demonstration. The camera zoomed in on a phalanx of police, helmeted and armed with translucent riot shields. They hurled commands at the protestors from behind their defensive fortifications. Just as the gulf between the protestors and police began to narrow, the coverage reverted to a blue screen. A thin band scrolled across the television apologizing for technical difficulties.

~

New and unfamiliar faces cycled in and out of the house. The number of security on patrol at any given time was doubled, and one couldn't turn a corner without confronting a deadpan sentinel with an automatic rifle over their shoulder. Mohadessi canceled our next scheduled interview, dispatching a handwritten note to my room. I witnessed several imposing figures in military fatigues enter the house, march single-file down the corridor, their boots resounding. I trailed them at a distance. They filed into Mohadessi's office. Demir, who received the officers, caught sight of me down the hall and closed the wooden door with a decisive thud.

I edited footage during the idle days, whittling down the hours of interviews. Editing was an exercise in patience. An early hero of mine, Orson Welles, said the "eloquence of film" was discovered in the editing room. But the footage I had captured felt static, rudderless, and starved of purpose. It was a body with no blood pulsing through its veins. Cadaverous. During the interviews, Mohadessi alternated between two settings: annoyed and aloof. Countless shots were ruined by the President checking his phone or looking up at the antique clock in his office.

The house still carried its air of secrecy. No televisions were turned on. Phones and radios were kept silent. My meals were—at the insistence of Chadli—taken privately in my room. I took an extended break from my morning swims and walks around the grounds. The simple act of passing someone in the hallway not on security detail seemed gauche, a breach of good manners.

~

"Pack your belongings," said one of the security personnel. He stood in the doorway of my open room. I had only seen him only once or twice before. He had a compact build and graying beard that belied his maturing age. Hasaam stood behind him, a half foot taller but clearly subordinate.

During my extended stay, I had become accustomed to sudden and half-formed commands. They were at this point standard practice.

"You have thirty minutes to get your things together," Hasaam said, sounding almost apologetic.

"Should I bring the camera equipment?"

The two men exchanged puzzled expressions and conferred with one another in terse whispers.

"It should be left here," the compact man said. He turned away, before pivoting back around. "Thirty minutes," he repeated.

I nodded to demonstrate my understanding. It was twenty minutes more than I needed.

~

Mohadessi insisted on a private jet that surpassed all others in luxury and function. (Even the bells and whistles had bells and whistles.) The seats swiveled at 180 degrees and were enfolded in Italian leather. The ceiling was affixed with an oversized, Art Deco-inspired light fixture that was wholly impractical for the space. It tolled during turbulence, and one had to duck and dodge simply to travel from one end of the cabin to the other.

I sat facing Mohadessi and the compact guard, who I learned was named Saad. He sat with perfect posture and an unnerving alertness. Zahra was in the rear of the aircraft with Hasaam, Demir, and several armed personnel.

Burdened by the silence, Mohadessi turned to Zahra: "I'm surprised you didn't wish to sit next to your friend," he said, nodding in my direction. Zahra made no acknowledgment of the comment. She picked up a magazine and began leafing through the well-worn pages.

Mohadessi was delighted by his cutting remark. The act of travel seemed to tease out his native cruelty.

"Where are we going?" I asked, finally.

Mohadessi prized open the can of seltzer in his seat holder. "Brussels," he said. "Have you been?"

"Once. A long time ago."

I turned and stared out the window at the wing of the plane, shearing through the sky like an open hand dragged through crystal clear water.

A private car deposited us in front of a grand hotel. Tall columns punctuated the lobby. Rounded skylights projected onto the marble floors shining pools of light. The lobby furniture was contemporary in style, with clean lines and cool, neutral tones. A caravan of porters, clad in navy blue livery, were tasked with carting our belonging upstairs and showing us to our rooms.

Hasaam and I were coupled together and assigned a suite a floor below the President and Zahra. I sat on the edge of the bed and took in my new surroundings. Hasaam began dutifully unpacking his clothing from his metallic suitcase: hanging starched shirts on hangers, delicately placing socks and underwear in dresser drawers. Once finished, he kicked off his shoes and unbuttoned his dress shirt, exposing a stained shirt underneath. He lay down on the bed. From the packet in his pocket, he shook loose a cigarette and sparked it with a cheap plastic lighter. He took a quick drag, followed by a long, slow exhale, both of us knowing full well this was a non-smoking room.

For dinner, Mohadessi had reserved a banquet room. The host, in his ironed finery, walked Hasaam and I through the main dining room to the private room in the back, where Mohadessi and Zahra were waiting. The security occupied a subordinate table in the corner of the room, like a far-flung planet at the solar system's recesses. I joined the head table. A laminated menu rested in Mohadessi's lap.

"I will say that the Belgians have less pretensions than the French," he said, still staring at his menu. "And better food. I will always prefer a mussel to a snail."

"I've never been a shellfish person," I said.

"Zahra and I vacationed in Bruges early in our marriage. What you might call a honeymoon. Do you remember?" he asked, turning to Zahra.

"I have a vague recollection."

A waiter came by to take our orders. I pointed blindly, a chicken dish of some kind. He complimented me on the order, perhaps mistaking me for a person of status whose favor was worthy of acquisition.

"I thought my early travels were a prelude to something greater," Mohadessi said. "One day you are a young man, blessed with a curiosity about the world. You imagine trekking through the Alps or swimming in the Ganges. Then you wake up and thirty years have passed and so much is left unexplored," Mohadessi said. He made a shrugging motion and took a drink of sparkling water.

Zahra looked amused by his sudden navel-gazing. She leaned back and rested her elbow on the shoulder of the chair.

"My advice to you, my boy: See the world while you still can," he said. "Before other duties lay claim to your time. That window is only open to us for so long."

"Excuse me."

I rose abruptly from the table, the napkin in my lap flopped to the floor. I headed toward the bathroom, which I had passed on the way into the restaurant. The bathroom was modern and austere. I ran the faucet and splashed several handfuls of water onto my face, before unspooling a square of paper towel and drying off.

It occurred to me that no one had shadowed me to the bathroom to stand outside the door. Rarely was I permitted to appear in public with the President—and never on neutral terrain. How easy it would be to walk through the front lobby and seize the freedom beyond the glass doors. A bird set loose from its cage. But how far could I expect to get on foot? I was a penniless man on foreign soil, without a friendly contact or phone to call the consulate. Even with a head start, the odds would never be in my favor. I took a deep breath, pushed open the bathroom door, and returned to the banquet room.

~

Hasaam watched soccer in the hotel room in his boxer shorts. Belgian clubs of middling ambitions playing in a league match. The President had not called or messaged, so Hasaam and I were left to wait in the hotel room, like extra clothing packed and later deemed unnecessary. I felt a familiar mix of boredom and unease that had carried with me through my time in captivity (if that was even the word to describe it).

Neither side could break through for the opening goal, stymied by well-organized defenses.

"Do you mind if I go for a swim?" I said.

Hasaam, unsure of whether he was in a position to reject the request, grudgingly replaced his pants and followed me down to the swimming pool. I proceeded to undress down to my underwear and slide into the temperature-controlled water. No one else was in the pool, nor were there any guests milling about or lounging on the deck. I swam several laps, slowed by a bodily torpor (my butterfly stroke was closer to a caterpillar). I heard a sudden chorus of cheers and floated to the edge of the pool. Hasaam was sitting upright on a reclining chair, watching the game on his phone.

"Liège scored," he said, mistaking my concern for curiosity.

~

Sanne and I traveled to Brussels. This was shortly after her second miscarriage and a year before we separated. We wanted to escape a feeling, a hardening dread, that we were tethered to one another out of familiarity, and no child could change that fact. The affection we once felt had turned to ember. We traveled from city to city, avoiding this truth, sitting silently at cafes, in bookshops, unwilling to face what had become painfully obvious—even to those who espied us from across a train car or passenger plane. We were people who had come asunder.

~

Hotel guests paused in front of the television in the breakfast area. A young man, bloodied and unsteady on his feet, his neckline doused in sweat, was dragged by soldiers into the back of a black military van. Spires of gray smoke rose behind him, as small clusters of people with cloth

128

handkerchiefs over their mouths staggered into the camera's view. The sound of concussion grenades were audible, even with the volume turned low (so as not to disturb the families in the dining room). The banner scrolling beneath the images carried a tally of people injured or dead. The latter figure numbering in the low hundreds. My eyes stayed wedded to the screen as impatient guests cut in front of me in line, piled their plates with sausage and bacon. On the way up the elevator, the yolk in my fried egg broke, pooling outward and submerging the rest of my breakfast.

~

Mohadessi was sitting at the bar, uncharacteristically hunched, his fingers drumming against the base of a champagne flute. An hour earlier a note had been slipped under my door, inviting me to join the President at the bar.

I had never seen him drink alcohol before, not so much as a glass of wine. I considered voicing this observation, but thought better of it, concerned that any remark would be seen as casting doubt on his religious discipline.

He patted the stool next to him. I ordered a top shelf scotch on the rocks. The drink came with a single, orbital ice cube rolling along the bottom of the glass.

"Sleep is a talent that diminishes with age," he said.

"I can relate to that sentiment."

"How have you enjoyed the city?"

"I haven't seen much of it."

"No?"

Mohadessi looked dismayed, as if my quarantine defied his direct instructions, and that my minders were meant to show me a good time.

"To be honest, I'm a bit unsettled by your indifference."

"In what sense?"

"The protests, the unrest," I said. "Are you not concerned at all? People are dying in the streets. More and more each day."

"This is not the first act of disloyalty I've witnessed. It certainly won't be the last," he said. "All children act out. This is natural. They need a stern father to set them straight."

I looked at him skeptically. Mohadessi stared at the bottles behind the bar, accosted by some distant thought or memory.

"The militants, they have no desire to lead. When power is in their grasp, they recoil. Their identity is in rebellion, in the act of resisting authority. It is all they know," he said. "Nothing terrifies them more than being in a position of power."

"And you have no fear of power, I take it."

"I do what has to be done. This is not like the civilized wars of the past. We live in a different time."

"Civilized war is a contradiction."

Mohadessi laughed.

"You think that you are principled, that you obey a moral code, but you deceive yourself. When your people ruled over my country, they were neither polite nor civilized."

"I don't defend the actions of my country."

Mohadessi swallowed the reminder of his flute and slid the glass forward.

"Do you not? I'm not sure you know what you stand for, Mr. Rai."

~

A fire alarm sounded early one morning. We emptied into the hallways and shuffled down the stairs, a great outpouring of life. I noticed some disregard the evacuation plan and take the elevators (the evacuation plan was, to be fair, a document that would have been read only by someone isolated for long hours in their room). Dozens of us funneled through the doors, angling for an expedited exit. The porters in the lobby tried in vain to marshal the masses. Outside, I looked around the growing arc of guests, many wrapped in plush hotel robes and slippers. They glowered and whispered to one another, crossed their arms over their chests. I searched for Mohadessi and Zahra, but they were absent from the crowd. After no more than fifteen minutes, the hotel manager told us it was safe to return to our rooms. They apologized for the inconvenience. Surly guests returned to the comfort of their beds. The emergency, we later learned from a loose-lipped concierge, was an admission of infidelity between a vacationing couple. The aggrieved party attempted to set their partner's clothing ablaze in the bathtub, but only succeeded in activating the alarms.

~

"If there's one thing that I've learned about myself, it's that I yearn for small comforts," Zahra said.

We were sharing a plate of Belgian fries, slathered in mayonnaise. Hasaam stood beside our table in the hotel restaurant. Enquiring diners may have wondered whether he was preparing to flambé a dessert or mash avocados in a bowl.

"The mayonnaise strikes me as strange, but then I remember we dip our fries in tomato paste and sugar," I said.

"You must miss your home."

132

"I've been itinerant for so long that I'm not sure I have a strong sense of home."

Zahra nodded, helped herself to another golden brown fry.

"Home, for most of us, is a security only known in childhood. After that, there are merely places where you rest your head for the night," she said. "If you ask me to think of home, I imagine I'm twelve years old again at our family house. We had a fig tree in the garden, and when they were ripe we would eat them with yogurt and honey."

"That sounds like a nice memory."

"It was."

She continued: "Lately I feel as though time is moving backwards. I'm remember people I haven't thought about for years. It's a curious thing. The contours of memory seem clearer than before."

A waiter bumped into Hasaam and dropped his empty tray. Hasaam stood over him menacingly as the man bent over and picked up the oversized disc.

"Let him be," Zahra said.

Hasaam stepped back obediently and assumed an air of practiced indifference.

I stared at the ceiling, as I had so many times in prison. The only thing different about the room was finer bathroom finishes. Hasaam muttered in his sleep, words and phrases at the margins of comprehension. My body was restless and couldn't settle in a position for longer than a few minutes. How many more days would we wait in purgatory? I considered the prospect of another week—or longer—in this dismal room. The others seemed unbothered, or at least put on a good face. Yet I feared what was to come. Once it was learned that Mohadessi had fled his country, the fighting would only intensify and the numbers scrolling underneath the news broadcast would rise.

~

The next morning I plunged for painted stones in the pool. I felt at ease with the mechanical undertaking, the water repelling my progress as I neared the pool floor. I set the colored rocks on the ledge and, once all of them were retrieved, scattered them again.

At the opposite end of the pool, a couple with brown skin like my own held their infant child in their arms.

The child splashed spasmodically in the shallow water. When the water sprayed his face, he paused to reconstitute himself before returning to the activity at hand.

I thought about the last time I had felt such excitement and curiosity. I couldn't remember. Time had become binary; its linear progress split into two halves. There was only before and after. Then and now.

The young couple looked in my direction and waved. The child made a noise of delight. I waved back at them. Behind me, a family member of theirs had entered the pool area.

~

Hasaam and I lounged on our beds and watched reruns of *Columbo*. Peter Falk was dubbed in French, but English subtitles made it possible to follow the arc of the story.

"Why does he act like a fool?" Hasaam asked. He was viewing the show for the first time.

"He pretends to be naïve, so the characters will let their guards down and say something incriminating," I explained. "It's a tactic."

"Such a waste of time. I would strike them with my fists until they gave up the information."

That, I said, was another tactic.

I found Demir in the hallway, looking at his watch, as if waiting for a sluggish train to announce itself.

"Are you waiting for someone?"

"Half my life is spent waiting," he said. "But behind every great man is someone with extraordinary patience."

A phone rang. Demir answered before the first bar of notes had finished chiming. He exchanged greetings with the caller in French, and then asked if the person was ready. He turned his back to me and recited a lengthy sequence of numbers. He repeated them for good measure and then paused for confirmation. The call ended with a perfunctory note of gratitude.

"You're moving his money," I said.

This knowledge seemed to pass telepathically from Demir's mind to my own. Without any hard evidence, I knew it to be a fact.

"We have to prepare for every eventuality," he said, sensing the uselessness of denial. He replaced his phone in his coat pocket.

"How will the people take it when they find out that Mohadessi has up and left, cleared out his accounts?"

"You're speaking on a topic you don't understand,

Mr. Rai," he said in an offhand tone. "There is a notable difference between divesting and diversifying. This is a simple matter of business."

Saad appeared beside me, silent as a feline.

"Would you help Mr. Rai back to his room? And tell Hasaam that it's time to switch assignments."

With a firm hand at my back, he walked me to my room. Moments later Hasaam was packing his belongings.

~

Saad—my new steward—seldom spoke. He demanded that I shower and shit with the door marginally ajar. Swimming in the pool was not allowed. Visiting the lobby for breakfast was not allowed. Drinking from the minibar was not allowed. Calling the front desk was not allowed. He watched no soccer matches, lit no cigarettes, consumed his coffee in one prolonged swallow. I asked him a litany of questions to which he rarely responded, and on the infrequent occasions when he did address me, he delivered the same two English words: *piss off*.

Zahra brought to my room a note, folded in quarters. She waited while Saad examined it, his eyebrows stitched together in disapproval. She wore a pea green rain coat and had an umbrella hooked over her forearm.

"Fine," Saad said. He went to the closet to retrieve his coat.

"I thought you could use a walk," she said, leaning forward to keep Saad from eavesdropping.

We walked along cobbled streets familiar to me from past visits. These were streets very much on the beaten track: lined with cafes, bars, and retail shops frequented by tourists. The mist thickened into a steady rain. Zahra thrust open her umbrella, the fabric modeled after early naturalist paintings.

"Thank you for the walk," I said.

"You don't need to thank me."

Young couples skirted us, arm in arm. Saad walked several yards behind, still smarting from being dragged on this unplanned excursion. We stopped at a café and sat outside under the striped red awning. Rain filtered off its sides. She ordered two cappuccinos. Saad, who sat at a neighboring table, declined to order anything, much to the server's displeasure.

"The last time I was here—in this city—was with my wife," I said. "That must have been a decade ago or longer."

"Do you think of her often?"

"Most days," I said, pausing. "I think about my mistakes. Because of her self-possessed nature, I assumed that little was needed of me. That I could drift in and out of the life we shared. I believed the distance was necessary to preserve our lifestyles as creative people. But that was a rationalization born out of fear."

"Fear of what?"

"Being found wanting."

Zahra palmed the small cappuccino cup with both hands, drawing from its warmth.

"She is an artist?"

"Yes, a pianist."

"I envy her," Zahra said. "To be young and gifted."

"Like me, she's not so young anymore."

"If you have more life ahead of you than behind you, then in my eyes you are young."

"Maybe in another life I will meet her again and get it right," I said.

"I think about this often. If different decisions might have led me to another outcome. Or if all choices bring me to the same place."

"It's impossible to say."

"You know I was pregnant once. Many years ago. I would dream about the ways her life would be different from my own."

"What happened?"

"It wasn't Mohadessi's child."

She finished her coffee. She had given what she was willing and would offer no more. I understood this. We sat for several minutes longer, watching pass before us a parade of parasoled couples, steeling themselves against the weather, their shoes slick with rain. Zahra paid for the coffees and we continued our walk.

Farther down the street, she paused and pointed with her umbrella.

"Let's stop in here," she said. The storefront was a rare and used bookstore. The windows were illuminated with lamp light, the genial glow of nostalgia. "We'll be no more than ten minutes," she said to Saad. His dissatisfaction was once again evident as he stood sentry outside.

"He hates the smell of old books," Zahra said as soon as he was out of earshot. "Won't step foot in the library at the house."

I browsed the towering shelves of books. Volumes were stacked in a chaotic fashion, as if a narrow storm front had just swept through. There was no pattern or logic to the layout. I followed her purposeful movements.

"The Collected Poems of Emily Dickinson," I said, pointing to careworn edition, balancing atop a plinth of lesser texts. Zahra made no recognition of the find. She took my arm in hers and guided me to the back of the store, beyond the frayed curtain separating the retail space from the storage area. The proprietor of the shop watched us pass, too weary to ask what we were searching for. She brought us to the back door, the delivery entrance. Before I could speak, she pressed a handwritten note and a hundred Euros into my palm.

"The address to your embassy," she said. "There is a car waiting around the corner. If you go now, they won't be able to reach you in time."

I stood there, immobilized, unable to process the rapid-fire instructions.

"You have to go."

She pushed open the door. The damp air accosted us. I felt my senses return to me.

"Come with me," I said

"I can't."

"They'll grant you asylum. There isn't a question."

She shook her head. A tear passed down the side of her cheek.

"I know where my place is."

I tried to appeal her decision, make a case for leaving with me, but no words came out.

"There isn't time for this. You have to go."

I was standing in the doorway. The rain beat against my back. Her hand was pressed to my chest, firm enough to keep me from stepping back inside.

I plunged the address and currency into my pocket and took a step backward. She shut the door, her eyes stained red. When I tried the door handle again, it was locked.

~

"Mr. Dolly will see you in a moment," the young man at reception said. This was one of three notices he had issued concerning Mr. Dolly's imminent arrival. I sat rigidly in the sea green accent chair, my right foot drumming against the hardwood floor. The door swayed open and appearing in the doorway was a bare-headed man in a limp gray suit.

"Come on in," he said. I took a seat in a leather chair, far more accommodating than the one in the waiting area. The room was unadorned, save for a folded American flag, framed and hung behind his desk. He had on his lapel a matching pin. Dolly struck me as a man with few interests beyond the daily intrigues of diplomatic work.

"Most of us thought you had died. Or worse, defected," he said, paging through a photocopied stack of papers. "This falls into the get-the-fuck-out-here category.

"You know who I am then?"

"Everyone does, Mr. Rai. Your face has been on everything short of milk cartons."

"I just want to go home."

"And you will. Naturally, we have a few questions for you. And you'll have to undergo an exam or two by our doctors. Assuming all goes as planned, we can rustle up a passport for you and have you on a flight home in no time."

Dolly put on a pair of reading glasses. He took a legal notepad from his desk, wet his thumb, and turned over the topmost page.

"Now, starting at the beginning, tell me what happened."

~

They settled me in a bedroom with spare furnishings: a single bed with a folded quilt at its foot, a small writing desk with a ladder-back chair, and a framed photograph of a former President of the United States (one of the more warring of the bunch) visiting the Embassy. The orientation of the room conveyed a message to its occupants, spelled out in bold type, which was not to get too comfortable. No matter how precarious your situation the powers that be could just as easily cast you back into the waiting arms of despots and death squads. Compassion was contingent on quotas, on quid prop quo, on the roll of a dice. It was a wonder anyone consigned to this room slept through the night.

~

The plane reached cruising altitude and the seatbelt sign flickered off. It was past midnight and a quarter of the passengers on the plane were asleep under thin acrylic blankets.

"A lot of people ask me how my plants stay in such good health," the older woman sitting next to me said. This was not a question I had asked. In fact, I hadn't uttered a single word to this person. "The secret is I talk to them every day. While I was gone, my grandson would put me on speakerphone and I would tell them stories about my trip."

I nodded my head reflexively. Her dyed hair looked like the head of a struck match.

"Were you traveling for business or leisure," she continued.

"Neither," I said, and that seemed to bring a welcome end to the line of questioning.

I picked up a magazine from the seat pouch in front of me. The crinkled copy flipped open to an article on a loosely recognizable television actor's favorite places to visit in Vancouver—the city where his new show was filmed. I returned the magazine to the pouch.

"Something to drink?" the airline attendant said. A rolling metal cart had materialized beside our row.

"Scotch on ice," I said. She turned the cap of the single-serve bottle until the seal snapped, poured the amber liquid into a plastic cup, and deposited the bottle in a bin underneath the cart.

"How much do I owe you?"

She winked. "Don't worry about it. It's on us."

~

Having slept for nineteen consecutive hours, I reconnected the landline phone (which I had pulled from the wall after a series of cold calls from enterprising journalists). I dialed Ali's number, referencing the notebook I kept of professional contacts. No answer. I left a message wishing him well and encouraging him to call me back as soon as he received the message. I tried Sunni and Naya at their home. The phone number was disconnected. I rechecked the number against my notebook, but no error had been made.

~

Nearly a week had passed and I still hadn't heard from Sunni or Ali. Jules, my agent, called and began speaking with an uncontained elation.

"I've had three calls this morning to option your story," she said.

"Nobody knows my story."

"They know the gist of it."

"No."

"I can get you an executive producer credit."

"Not interested."

"Think of the projects you can finance with the money. No more groveling to rich white hedge funders who want a trophy for their guest bathrooms."

I went quiet on the line.

"Think about it. But think quickly. All it takes is for Sean Penn to get kidnapped by a Colombian cartel for you to get knocked off your perch."

"Bye."

I hung up the phone.

~

Jules had worn me down (or—more truthfully—I had worn myself down), and I agreed to a battery of lunch meetings and studio visits in Los Angeles. I even had an early dinner scheduled with Sanne, who was passing through on her way to a wedding in San Francisco.

I checked my flight time on the departure screen: the plane was on time. With a few minutes to spare before boarding, I bought a cup of coffee and a newspaper from a nearby kiosk. I returned to the waiting area and opened the paper. Buried beneath stories on the upcoming midterm elections was a condensed article—no more than a couple hundred words—from the paper's foreign correspondent: *Wife of President Mohammed Mohadessi Suspected Missing.* The correspondent's unnamed source claimed she had disappeared days after Mohadessi's military quelled the uprisings and regained control of the region. She hadn't been seen publicly in weeks, though precise details were sparse.

I dumped the coffee in the garbage and bought a copy of every newspaper for purchase at the kiosk. The story was only covered in one other paper and the particulars were even less defined. I removed my laptop from its bag and began combing every news website, gossip rag, and social media feed I knew. A handful of international outlets had been monitoring the story, but everything I came across was limited in its details. Mohadessi's administration was mum. They had started clamping down on dissident activity. No official statement had been issued on the matter.

The flight announced final boarding, but I was already bounding for the exits.

~

A letter from Brussels arrived in the mail, backdated. Its appearance produced a terrible unease, and I waited a day before opening it. Inside the envelope was a photograph, decades old and brittle with wear. A young girl in a plaid uniform was smiling at the camera, a pronounced gap between her two front teeth. This was Zahra. Beside her, a girl several years older, blessed with the early trappings of beauty, rested a crooked arm on the young girl's shoulder. In the background, a fig tree was primed for picking. I turned over the photograph.

My sister, Saffiyah, and I. This picture has been with me during times of great joy and great sadness. I don't remember

where it was taken, or what occasion it marked. There is so
much I don't know, and for once I am fine with that unknowing.

Zahra

I looked at the photograph for several moments longer before slipping it back into the brown paper envelope.

For months I waited for a successive letter, the assurance of safety. It never arrived. I checked the news compulsively, but they had moved onto more marketable stories. My contacts in the country had become unresponsive. Fear had strong-armed them into silence. My doctor referred me to a therapist specializing in post-traumatic stress. His waiting room smelled of cheap candles and drying paint. After several unproductive sessions, I stopped returning. During the days, I spent hours at the public library researching topics for a new project, but no subject I studied or book I read stirred my interest. I attended lunch meetings with producers, only to realize that they were less interested in my ideas than having me recount my story, so they could repeat it at future business luncheons and social functions. I met a young woman, a lawyer for undocumented families, who offered her company at a trying time. We were set up by a mutual friend who wrote plays of an absurdist variety. She worked at a bakery to pay her way through law school, and her apartment was often warm with fresh breads and pastries. In time, I moved in and the apartment became a space we shared together. It was different than it was with Sanne—not without passion, but our relationship seemed to hum at a quieter volume. Insomnia was a lingering symptom of my internment, and on the nights when I couldn't beckon sleep, I stared at the ceiling in our bedroom and imagined Zahra on the bright shores of the French Riviera or among the cherry blossoms of Kyoto or journeying through the arid deserts of the Australian Outback. Bracing herself against the wind, unshrinking.

ACKNOWLEDGMENTS

My deepest gratitude to the friends and family members who supported me in innumerable ways through the writing of this book. Thank you to t thilleman and the Spuyten Duyvil team for believing in it. And thank you to MASS MoCA, Blue Mountain Center, and the Constance Saltonstall Foundation for the Arts for the gift of time, space, and community.

RAVI MANGLA is the author of the novel *Understudies* (Outpost19). His writing has appeared in The Kenyon Review, Cincinnati Review, American Short Fiction, Jacobin, and The Paris Review Daily. He lives in Western New York and works as a political organizer.

CPSIA information can be obtained
at www.ICGtesting.com
Printed in the USA
LVHW091546030423
743334LV00005B/686

9 781956 005585